Mathilde Blind

Dramas in Miniature

With a front. by Ford Madox Brown

Mathilde Blind

Dramas in Miniature
With a front. by Ford Madox Brown

ISBN/EAN: 9783337142452

Printed in Europe, USA, Canada, Australia, Japan

Cover: Foto ©Andreas Hilbeck / pixelio.de

More available books at **www.hansebooks.com**

BY

MATHILDE BLIND

WITH A FRONTISPIECE BY FORD MADOX BROWN

London
CHATTO & WINDUS, PICCADILLY
1891

CONTENTS.

DRAMAS IN MINIATURE.

LYRICS.

DRAMAS IN MINIATURE.

E

THE RUSSIAN STUDENT'S TALE.

THE midnight sun with phantom glare
Shone on the soundless thoroughfare
Whose shuttered houses, closed and still,
Seemed bodies without heart or will ;
Yea, all the stony city lay
Impassive in that phantom day,
As amid livid wastes of sand
The sphinxes of the desert stand.

  * * * * *

And we, we two, turned night to day,
As, whistling many a student's lay,
We sped along each ghostly street,
With girls whose lightly tripping feet

Well matched our longer, stronger stride,
In hurrying to the water-side.
We took a boat ; each seized an oar,
And put his will into each stroke,
Until on either hand the shore
Slipped backwards, as our voices woke
Far echoes, mingling like a dream
With swirl and tumult of the stream.
On—on—away, beneath the ray
Of midnight in the mask of day ;
By great wharves where the masts at peace
Look like the ocean's barren trees ;
Past palaces and glimmering towers,
And gardens fairy-like with flowers,
And parks of twilight green and closes,
The very Paradise of roses.
The waters flow ; on, on we row,
Now laughing loud, now whispering low ;
And through the splendour of the white
Electrically glowing night,

Wind-wafted from some perfumed dell,

Tumultuously there loudly rose

Above the Neva's surge and swell,

With amorous ecstasies and throes,

And lyric spasms of wildest wail,

The love-song of a nightingale.

* * * * *

I see her still beside me.   Yea,

As if it were but yesterday,

I see her—see her as she smiled ;

Her face that of a little child

For innocent sweetness undefiled ;

And that pathetic flower-like blue

Of eyes which, as they looked at you,

Seemed yet to stab your bosom through.

I rowed, she steered ; oars dipped and flashed,

The broadening river roared and splashed,

So that we hardly seemed to hear

Our comrades' voices, though so near ;

Their faces seeming far away,

As still beneath that phantom day
I looked at her, she smiled at me!
And then we landed—I and she.

  *   *   *   *   *

There's an old Café in the wood ;
A students' haunt on summer eves,
Round which responsive poplar leaves
Quiver to each æolian mood
Like some wild harp a poet smites
On visionary summer nights.
I ordered supper, took a room
Green-curtained by the tremulous gloom
Of those fraternal poplar trees
Shaking together in the breeze ;
My pulse, too, like a poplar tree,
Shook wildly as she smiled at me.
Eye in eye, and hand in hand,
Awake amid the slumberous land,
I told her all my love that night—
How I had loved her at first sight ;

How I was hers, and seemed to be
Her own to all eternity.
And through the splendour of the white
Electrically glowing night,
Wind-wafted from some perfumed dell,
Tumultuously there loudly rose
Above the Neva's surge and swell,
With amorous ecstasies and throes,
And lyric spasms of wildest wail,
The love-song of a nightingale.

    *   *   *   *   *

I see her still beside me.   Yea,
As if it were but yesterday,
I hear her tell with cheek aflame
Her ineradicable shame—
So sweet a flower in such vile hands!
Oh, loved and lost beyond recall!
Like one who hardly understands,
I heard the story of her fall.
The odious barter of her youth,

Of beauty, innocence, and truth,

Of all that honest women hold

Most sacred—for the sake of gold.

A weary seampstress, half a child,

Left unprotected in the street,

Where, when so hungry, you would meet

All sorts of tempters that beguiled.

Oh, infamous and senseless clods,

Basely to taint so pure a heart,

And make a maid fit for the gods

A creature of the common mart!

She spoke quite simply of things vile—

Of devils with an angel's face;

It seemed the sunshine of her smile

Must purify the foulest place.

She told me all—she would be true—

Told me of things too sad, too bad;

And, looking in her eyes' clear blue

My passion nearly drove me mad!

I tried to speak, but tried in vain;

A sob rose to my throat as dry
As ashes—for between us twain
A murdered virgin seemed to lie.
And through the splendour of the white
Electrically glowing night,
Wind-wafted from some perfumed dell,
Tumultuously there loudly rose
Above the Neva's surge and swell,
With amorous ecstasies and throes,
And lyric spasms of wildest wail,
The love-song of a nightingale.

  *   *   *   *   *

Poor craven creature!   What was I,
To sit in judgment on her life,
Who dared not make this child my wife,
And lift her up to love's own sky?
This poor lost child we all—yes, all—
Had helped to hurry to her fall,
Making a social leper of
God's creature consecrate to love.

I looked at her—she smiled no more ;
She understood it all before
A syllable had passed my lips ;
And like a horrible eclipse,
Which blots the sunlight from the skies,
A blankness overspread her eyes—
The blankness as of one who dies.
I knew how much she loved me—knew
How pure and passionately true
Her love for me, which made her tell
What scorched her like the flames of hell.
And I, I loved her too, so much,
So dearly, that I dared not touch
Her lips that had been kissed in sin ;
But with a reverential thrill
I took her work-worn hand and thin,
And kissed her fingers, showing still
Where needle-pricks had marred the skin.
And, ere I knew, a hot tear fell,
Scalding the place which I had kissed,

As between clenching teeth I hissed
Our irretrievable farewell.
And through the smouldering glow of night,
Mixed with the shining morning light
Wind-wafted from some perfumed dell,
Above the Neva's surge and swell,
With lyric spasms, as from a throat
Which dying breathes a faltering note,
There faded o'er the silent vale
The last sob of a nightingale.

THE MYSTIC'S VISION.

I.

Ah! I shall kill myself with dreams!
   These dreams that softly lap me round
Through trance-like hours, in which, meseems,
   That I am swallowed up and drowned;
Drowned in your love which flows o'er me
As o'er the seaweed flows the sea.

II.

In watches of the middle night,
   'Twixt vesper and 'twixt matin bell,
With rigid arms and straining sight,
   I wait within my narrow cell;
With muttered prayers, suspended will,
I wait your advent—statue-still.

III.

Across the Convent garden walls
　　The wind blows from the silver seas ;
Black shadow of the cypress falls
　　Between the moon-meshed olive trees ;
Sleep-walking from their golden bowers,
Flit disembodied orange flowers.

IV.

And in God's consecrated house,
　　All motionless from head to feet,
My heart awaits her heavenly Spouse,
　　As white I lie on my white sheet ;
With body lulled and soul awake,
I watch in anguish for your sake.

V.

And suddenly, across the gloom,
　　The naked moonlight sharply swings ;

A Presence stirs within the room,

    A breath of flowers and hovering wings :

Your Presence without form and void,

Beyond all earthly joys enjoyed.

VI.

My heart is hushed, my tongue is mute,

    My life is centred in your will ;

You play upon me like a lute

    Which answers to its master's skill,

Till passionately vibrating,

Each nerve becomes a throbbing string.

VII.

Oh, incommunicably sweet !

    No longer aching and apart,

As rain upon the tender wheat,

    You pour upon my thirsty heart ;

As scent is bound up in the rose,

Your love within my bosom glows.

VIII.

Unseen, untouched, unheard, unknown,
　You take possession of your bride ;
I lose myself to live alone
　In you, who once were crucified
For me, that now would die in you,
As in the sun a drop of dew.

IX.

Fish may not perish in the deep,
　Nor sparrows fall through yielding air,
Pure gold in hottest flame will keep ;
　How should I fail and falter where
You are, O Lord, in whose control
For ever lies my living soul ?

X.

Ay, break through every wall of sense,
　And pierce my flesh as nails did pierce

Your bleeding limbs in anguish tense,

And torture me with bliss so fierce,

That self dies out, as die it must,

Ashes to ashes, dust to dust.

XI.

Thus let me die, so loved and lost,

Annihilated in my dreams !

Nor force me, an unwilling ghost,

To face the loud day's brutal beams ;

The noisy world's inanities,

All vanity of vanities.

THE MESSAGE.

FROM side to side the sufferer tossed
  With quick impatient sighs ;
Her face was bitten as by frost,
The look as of one hunted crossed
  The fever of her eyes.

All scared she seemed with life and woe,
  Yet scarcely could have told
More than a score of springs or so ;
Her hair had girlhood's morning glow,
  And yet her mouth looked old.

Not long for her the sun would rise,
  Nor that young slip of moon,

C

Wading through London's smoky skies,
Would dwindling meet those dwindling eyes,
   Ere May was merged in June.

May was it somewhere?   Who, alas!
   Could fancy it was May?
For here, instead of meadow grass,
You saw, through naked panes of glass,
   Bare walls of whitish gray.

Instead of songs, where in the quick
   Leaves hide the blackbirds' nests,
You heard the moaning of the sick,
And tortured breathings harsh and thick
   Drawn from their labouring chests.

She muttered, "What's the odds to me?"
   With an old cynic's sneer;
And looking up, cried mockingly,
"I hate you, nurse!   Why, can't you see
   You'll make no convert here?"

And then she shook her fist at Heaven,
   And broke into a laugh!
Yes, though her sins were seven times seven,
Let others pray to be forgiven—
   She scorned such canting chaff.

Oh, it was dreadful, sir! Far worse
   In one so young and fair;
Sometimes she'd scoff and swear and curse;
Call me bad names, and vow each nurse
   A fool for being there.

And then she'd fall back on her bed,
   And many a weary hour
Would lie as rigid as one dead;
Her white throat with the golden head
   Like some torn lily flower.

We could do nothing, one and all
   How much we might beseech;

Her girlish blood had turned to gall :
Far lower than her body's fall
   Her soul had sunk from reach.

Her soul had sunk into a slough
   Of evil past repair.
The world had been against her ; now
Nothing in heaven or earth should bow
   Her stubborn knees in prayer.

Yet I felt sorry all the same,
   And sometimes, when she slept,
With head and hands as hot as flame,
I watched beside her, half in shame,
   Smoothed her bright hair and wept.

To die like this—'twas awful, sir !
   To know I prayed in vain ;
And hear her mock me, and aver
That if her life came back to her
   She'd live her life again.

Was she a wicked girl ?   What then ?
    She didn't care a pin !
She was not worse than all those men
Who looked so shocked in public, when
    They made and shared her sin.

"Shut up, nurse, do !   Your sermons pall ;
    Why can't you let me be ?
Instead of worrying o'er my fall,
I wish, just wish, you sisters all
    Turned to the likes of me."

I shuddered !   I could bear no more,
    And left her to her fate ;
She was too cankered at the core ;
Her heart was like a bolted door,
    Where Love had knocked too late.

I left her in her savage spleen,
    And hoarsely heard her shout,

"What does the cursed sunlight mean
By shining in upon this scene?
  Oh, shut the sunlight out!"

Sighing, I went my round once more,
  Full heavy for her sin;
Just as Big Ben was striking four,
The sun streamed through the open door,
  As a young girl came in.

She held a basket full of flowers—
  Cowslip and columbine;
A lilac bunch from rustic bowers,
Strong-scented after morning showers,
  Smelt like some cordial wine.

There, too, peeped Robin-in-the-hedge,
  There daisies pearled with dew,
Wild parsley from the meadow's edge,
Sweet-william and the purple vetch,
  And hyacinth's heavenly blue.

But best of all the spring's array,
  Green boughs of milk-white thorn ;
Their petals on each perfumed spray
Looked like the wedding gift of May
  On nature's marriage morn.

And she who bore those gifts of grace
  To our poor patients there,
Passed like a sunbeam through the place :
Dull eyes grew brighter for her face,
  Angelically fair.

She went the round with elf-like tread,
  And with kind words of cheer,
Soothing as balm of Gilead,
Laid wild flowers on each patient's bed,
  And made the flowers more dear.

At last she came where Nellie Dean
  Still moaned and tossed about—

" What does the cursed sunlight mean
By shining in upon this scene ?
  Will no one shut it out ? "

And then she swore with rage and pain,
  And moaning tried to rise ;
It seemed her ugly words must stain
The child who stood with heart astrain,
  And large blue listening eyes.

Her fair face did not blush or bleach,
  She did not shrink away ;
Alas! she was beyond the reach
Of sweet or bitter human speech—
  Deaf as the flowers of May.

Only her listening eyes could hear
  That hardening in despair,
Which made that other girl, so near
In age to her, a thing to fear
  Like fever-tainted air.

She took green boughs of milk-white thorn
   And laid them on the sheet,
Whispering appealingly, "Don't scorn
My flowers! I think, when one's forlorn,
   They're like a message, Sweet."

How heavenly fresh those blossoms smelt,
   Like showers on thirsty ground!
The sick girl frowned as if repelled,
And with hot hands began to pelt
   And fling them all around.

But then some influence seemed to stay
   Her hands with calm control;
Her stormy passion cleared away,
The perfume of the breath of May
   Had passed into her soul.

A nerve of memory had been thrilled,
   And, pushing back her hair,

She stretched out hungry arms half filled
With flower and leaf, and panting shrilled,
  "Where are you, mother, where?"

And then her eyes shone darkly bright
  Through childhood in a mist,
As if she suddenly caught sight
Of some one hidden in the light
  And waited to be kissed.

"Oh, mother dear!" we heard her moan,
  "Have you not gone away?
I dreamed, dear mother, you had gone,
And left me in the world alone,
  In the wild world astray.

"It was a dream; I'm home again!
  I hear the ivy-leaves
Tap-tapping on the leaded pane!
Oh, listen! how the laughing rain
  Runs from our cottage eaves!

" How very sweet the things do smell!
    How bright our pewter shines!
I am at home ; I feel so well :
I think I hear the evening bell
    Above our nodding pines.

" The firelight glows upon the brick,
    And pales the rising moon ;
And when your needles flash and click,
My heart, my heart, that felt so sick,
    Throbs like a hive in June.

" If only father would not stay
    And gossip o'er his brew ;
Then, reeling homewards, lose his way,
Come staggering in at break of day
    And beat you black and blue!

" Yet he can be as good as gold,
    When mindful of the farm,

He tills the field and tends the fold :
But never fear ; when I'm grown old
   I'll keep him out of harm.

" And then we'll be as happy here
   As kings upon their throne !
I dreamed you'd left me, mother dear ;
That you lay dead this many a year
   Beneath the churchyard stone.

" Mother, I sought you far and wide,
   And ever in my dream,
Just out of reach you seemed to hide ;
I ran along the streets and cried,
   ' Where are you, mother, where ? '

" Through never-ending streets in fear
   I ran and ran forlorn ;
And through the twilight yellow-drear
I saw blurred masks of loafers leer,
   And point at me in scorn.

" How tired, how deadly tired, I got ;

   I ached through all my bones !

The lamplight grew one quivering blot,

And like one rooted to the spot,

   I dropped upon the stones.

" A hard bed make the stones and cold,

   The mist a wet, wet sheet ;

And in the mud, like molten gold,

The snaky lamplight blinking rolled

   Like guineas at my feet.

" Surely there were no mothers when

   A voice hissed in my ear,

' A sovereign ! Quick ! Come on !'—and then

A knowing leer !   There were but men,

   And not a creature near.

" I went—I could not help it.   Oh,

   I didn't want to die !

With now a kiss and now a blow,

Strange men would come, strange men would go ;

 I didn't care—not I.

" Sometimes my life was like a tale

 Read in a story-book ;

Our blazing nights turned daylight pale,

Champagne would fizz like ginger-ale,

 Red wine flow like a brook.

" Then like a vane my dream would veer :

 I walked the street again ;

And through the twilight yellow-drear

Blurred clouds of faces seemed to peer,

 And drift across the rain."

She started with a piercing scream

 And wildly rolling eye :

" Ah me ! it was no evil dream

To pass with the first market-team—

 That thing of shame am I.

" Where were you that you could not come ?

　Were you so far above—

Far as the moon above a slum ?

Yet, mother, you were all the sum

　I had of human love.

" Ah yes ! you've sent this branch of May,

　A fair light from the past.

The town is dark—I went astray.

Forgive me, mother !   Lead the way ;

　I'm going home at last."

In eager haste she tried to rise,

　And struggled up in bed,

With luminous, transfigured eyes,

As if they glassed the opening skies,

　Fell back, sir, and was dead.

A MOTHER'S DREAM.

I.

THE snow was falling thick and fast
    On Christmas Eve ;
Across the heath the distant blast
Wailed wildly like a soul in grief,
A waste soul or a windy leaf
Whirled round and round without reprieve,
    And lost at last.

II.

Lisa woke shivering from her sleep
    At break of day,
And felt her flesh begin to creep.

"My child, my child!" she cried; "now may
Our blessed Lord, whose hand doth stay
The wild-fowl on their trackless way,
    Thee guard and keep."

III.

"Dreams! dreams!" she to herself did say,
    And shook with fright.
"I saw her plainly where I lay
Fly past me like a flash of light;
Fly out into the wintry night,
Out in the snow as snowy white,
    Far, far away.

IV.

"Her cage hung empty just above
    Your chair, *ma mie;*
Empty as is my heart of love

D

Since you, my child, dwell far from me—
Dwell in the convent over sea ;
All of you left to love Marie,
    Your darling dove."

V.

Hark to that fond, familiar coo !
    Oh, joy untold !
It falls upon her heart like dew.
There safely perching as of old,
The dove is calling through the cold
And ghastly dawn o'er wood and wold,
    " Coo-whoo ! Coo-whoo !"

VI.

The snow fell softly, flake by flake,
    This Christmas Day,
And whitened every bush and brake ;

And o'er the hills so ashen gray
The wind was wailing far away,
Was wailing like a child astray
    Whose heart must break.

VII.

"I miss my child," she wailed ; "I miss
      Her everywhere !
That's why I have such dreams as this.
I miss her step upon the stair,
I miss her laughter in the air,
I miss her bonnie face and hair,
    And oh—her kiss !

VIII.

"Christmas ! Last Christmas, oh how fleet,
    With lark-like trill,
She danced about on fairy feet !

Her eyes clear as a mountain rill,

Where the blue sky is lingering still ;

Her rosebud lips the dove would bill

　　For something sweet.

IX.

" My dove ! my dear ! my undefiled !

　　Oh, heavy doom !

My life has left me with the child.

She was a sunbeam in my room,

She was a rainbow on the gloom,

She was the wild rose on a tomb

　　Where weeds run wild.

X.

" And yet—'tis better thus ! 'Tis best,

　　They tell me so.

Yes, though my heart is like a nest,

Whence all the little birds did go—
An empty nest that's full of snow—
Let me take all the wail and woe,
    So she be blest.

XI.

" Let me take all the sin and shame,
    And weep for two,
That she may bear no breath of blame.
'Sin—sin!' they say; what sin had you,
Pure as the dawn upon the dew?
Child—robbed of a child's rightful due,
    Her father's name.

XII.

" I gave her life to live forlorn !
    Oh, let that day
Be darkness wherein I was born !

Let not God light it, let no ray

Shine on it; let it turn away

Its face, because my sin must weigh

    Her down with shame.

XIII.

"I?   I?   Was I the sinner?   I,

    Not *he*, they say,

Who told me, looking eye in eye,

We'd wed far North where grand and gray

His fair ancestral castle lay,

Amid the woods of Darnaway—

    And told a lie.

XIV.

" But I was young ; and in my youth

    I simply thought

That English gentlemen spoke truth,

Even to a Norman maid, who wrought
The blush-rose shells the tide had brought
To fairy toys which children bought
     Before my booth.

XV.

" 'Those fairy fingers,' he would say,
     'With shell-pink nails,
Shall shame the pearls of Darnaway'"
And in his yacht with swelling sails
We flew before the favouring gales,
Where leagues on leagues his woods and vales
     Stretched dim and gray.

XVI.

" Grim rose his castle o'er the wood ;
     Its hoary halls
Frowned o'er the Findhorn's roaring flood ;

Where, winged with spray and water-galls,
The headlong torrent leaps and falls
In thunder through its tunnelled walls,
    Streaked as with blood."

XVII.

It all came back in one wild flash
    Of cruel light,
And memory smote her like a lash :—
The foolish trust, the fond delight,
The helpless rage, the fevered flight,
The feet that dragged on through the night,
    The torrent's splash.

XVIII.

The long, long sickness bred of lies
    And lost belief ;
The short, sharp pangs and shuddering sighs ;

The new-born babe, that in her grief
Bore her wrecked spirit such relief
As the dove-carried olive-leaf
    To Noah's eyes.

XIX.

It all came back, and lit her soul
    With lurid flame;
How she—she—she—from whom he stole
Her virgin love and honest name—
Must, for the ailing child's sake, tame
Her pride, and take—oh, shame of shame!—
    His lordship's dole.

XX.

Like one whom grief hath driven wild,
    She cried again,
" My snowdrop shall not be defiled,

Nor catch the faintest soil or stain,

Reared in the shadow of my pain!

How should a guilty mother train

    A guiltless child?

XXI.

"You shall be spotless, you!" said she,

    "Whate'er my woe;

Even as the snow on yonder lea.

You shall be spotless!"   Faint and low,

The wind in dying seemed to blow,

To breathe across the hills of snow,

    "Marie! Marie!"

XXII.

A voice was calling far away,

    O'er fields and fords,

Across the Channel veiled and gray;

A voice was calling without words,
Touching her nature's deepest chords ;
Drawing her, drawing her as with cords —
    She might not stay.

XXIII.

Uprose the sun and still and round,
    Shorn of his heat,
Glared bloodshot o'er the frosty ground,
As down the shuttered village street
Fast, fast walked Lisa, and her feet
Left black tracks in earth's winding-sheet
    And made no sound.

XXIV.

Then on, on, by the iron way—
    With whistling scream—
Piercing hard rocks like potter's clay,

She flashed as in a shifting dream
Through flying town, o'er flowing stream,
Borne on by mighty wings of steam,
    Away, away.

XXV.

A sound of wind, and in the air
    The sea-gull's screech,
And waves lap-lapping everywhere ;
A rush of ropes and volleyed speech,
And white cliffs sinking out of reach,
Then rising on the rival beach,
    Boulogne-sur-Mer.

XXVI.

Above the ramparts on the hill,
    Whence like a chart
It saw the low land spreading chill,

Within its cloistered walls apart
The Convent of the Sacred Heart
Rose o'er the noise of street and mart,
 Serenely still.

XXVII.

Above the unquiet sea it rose,
 A quiet nest,
Severed from earthly wants and woes.
There might the weary find his rest ;
There might the pilgrim cease his quest ;
There might the soul with guilt oppressed
 Implore repose.

XXVIII.

The day was done, the sun dropped low
 Behind the mill
That swung within its blood-red glow ;

And up the street and up the hill
Lisa walked fast and faster still,
Her sable shadow lengthening chill
    Across the snow.

XXIX.

Hark ! heavenly clear, with holy swell,
    She hears elate
The greeting of the vesper bell,
And, knocking at the convent gate,
Sighs, " Here she prays God early and late ;
Walled in from love, walled in from hate ;
    All's well ! All's well ! "

XXX.

A sweat broke from her every pore,
    And yet she smiled,
As, stumbling through the clanging door,

She faced a nun of aspect mild.
Like some starved wolf's her eyes gleamed wild :
" My child!" she gasped ; " I want my child."
    And nothing more.

XXXI.

The nun looked at her, shocked to see
    The violent sway
Of love's unbridled agony ;
And calmly queried on the way,
" Your child, Madame ?   What child, I pray ? "
Still, still the mother could but say,
    " Marie !   Marie ! "

XXXII.

The nun in silence bowed her head,
    And then aloud,
" Christ Jesus knows our needs," she said.

" Madame, far from the sinful crowd,
The maiden to the Lord you vowed ;
There is no safeguard like a shroud—
    Your child is dead.

XXXIII.

" Upon the night Christ saw the light
    She passed away,
As snow will when the sun shines bright.
We heard her moaning where she lay,
' Come, mother, come, while yet you may ; '
Then like a dove, at break of day,
    Her soul took flight."

XXXIV.

As from a blow the mother fell,
    No moan made she ;
They bore her to the little cell :

There in her coffin lay Marie,

Spotless as snow upon the lea,

Beautiful exceedingly :

      All's well !   All's well !

A CARNIVAL EPISODE.

NICE, '87.

I.

WE two there together alone in the night,
　Where its shadow unconsciously bound us ;
My beautiful lady all shrouded in white,
She and I looking down from the balcony's height
On the maskers below in the flickering light,
　As they revelled and rioted round us.

II.

Such a rush, such a rage, and a rapture of life
　Such shouts of delight and of laughter,

On the quays that I watched with the General's
    wife ;
Such a merry-go-reeling of figures was rife,
Turning round to the tune of gay fiddle and fife,
    As if never a morning came after.

III.

The houses had emptied themselves in the streets,
    Where the maskers bombarded each other
With a shower of confetti and hailstorm of
    sweets
Till the pavements were turning the colour of
    sheets ;
Where a prince will crack jokes with a pauper he
    meets,
    For the time like a man and a brother.

IV.

The Carnival frolic was now at its height ;
    The whole population in motion

Stood watching the swift constellations of light
That crackling flashed up on their arrowy flight,
Then spreading their fairy-like fires on the night,
  Fell in luminous rain on the ocean.

V.

And now and again the quick dazzle would flare,
  Glowing red on black masks and white dresses.
We two there together drew back from the glare ;
Drew in to the room, and her hood unaware
Fell back from the plaits of her opulent hair,
  That uncoiled the brown snakes of its tresses.

VI.

How fatally fair was my lady, my queen,
  As that wild light fell round her in flashes ;
How fatally fair with that mutinous mien,
And those velvety hands all alive with the sheen
Of her rings, and her eyes that were narrowed
      between
    Heavy lids darkly laced with long lashes !

VII.

Almost I hated her beauty! The air
  I was breathing seemed steeped in her presence.
How maddening that waltz was! Ah, how came
    I there
Alone with that woman so fatally fair,
With the scent of her garments, the smell of her
    hair,
  Passing into my blood like an essence?

VIII.

Her eyes seemed to pluck at the roots of my
    heart,
  And to put all my blood in a fever;
My soul was on fire, my veins seemed to start,
To hold her, to fold her but once to my heart,
I'd have willingly bared my broad chest to the
    dart,
  And been killed, ay, and damned too for ever.

IX.

I forgot, I forgot!—oh, disloyal, abhorred,
    With the spell of her eyes on my eyes—
That her husband, the man of all men I adored,
Might be fighting for us at the point of the sword ;
Might be killing or killed by an African horde,
    Afar beneath African skies.

X.

I forgot—nay, I cared not! What cared I to-night
    For aught but my lady, my love,
As she toyed with her mask in the flickering light,
Then suddenly dropped it, perchance, at the sight
Of my passion now reaching its uttermost height,
    As a tide with the full moon above!

XI.

Yet I knew, though I loved her so madly, I knew
    She was only just playing her game.

She would toy with my heart all the Carnival
    through ;
She would turn to a traitor a man who was true ;
She would drain him of love and then break him
    in two,
  And wash her white hands of his shame.

XII.

Yet beware, O my beautiful lady, beware !
  You must cure me of love or else kill.
That fire burns longest that's slowest to flare :
My love is a force that will force you to care ;
Nay, I'll strangle us both in the ropes of your
    hair
  Should you dream you can drop me at will.

XIII.

And then—how I know not—delirious delight !
  Her lips were pressed close upon mine ;

My arms clung about her as when in affright
Wrecked men cling to spars in a tempest at
    night ;
So madly I clung to her, crushed her with might
   To my heart which her heart made divine.

XIV.

Oh, merciful Heavens !   What drove us apart
   With a shudder of sundering lives ?
Oh, was it the throb of my passionate heart
That made the doors tremble, the windows to
    start ;
Or was it my lady just playing her part,
   Most indignant, most outraged of wives ?

XV.

She was white as the chalk in the streets—was she
    fain
   To turn on me now with a sneer ?

All the blood in my body surged up to my
    brain,
And my heart seemed half bursting with passion
    and pain,
As I seized her slim hands—but I dropped them
    again !
    Ah ! treason is mother to fear.

XVI.

Had it come upon us at that magical hour,
    The judgment of God the Most High ?
The floor 'gan to heave and the ceiling to lower,
The dead walls to start with malevolent power,
Till your hair seemed to rise and your spirit to
    cower,
    As the very stones shook with a sigh.

XVII.

" With you in my arms let the world crack asunder ;
    Let us die, love, together !" I cried.

Then, then with a clatter and boom as of thunder,
A beam crashed between us and drove us asunder,
And all things rocked round us, above us and
    under,
  Like a boat that is rocked on a tide.

XVIII.

She sprang like a greyhound—no greyhound more
    fleet—
  And ran down the staircase in motion ;
And blindly I followed her into the street,
All choked up with people in panic retreat
From the houses that scattered their plaster like
    sleet
  On the crowd in bewildered commotion.

XIX.

Black masks and white dominoes, hale men and
    dying,
  Scared women that shook as with fever

Poor babes in their bedgowns all piteously crying,

Tiles hurled from the housetops—all flying, all
    flying,

As I, wild with passion, implored her with sighing

    To fly with me now and for ever.

XX.

" Go, go!" and she waved me away as she spoke,

    Carried on by the crowd like a feather ;

" You forget that it was but a Carnival joke.

Now blest be the terrible earthquake that broke

In between you and me, and has saved at a stroke

    Us two in the night there together."

THE BATTLE OF FLOWERS.

I.

THE battle raged, no blood was spilled,
　　Though missiles flew in showers ;
Hard though they hit, they never killed
　　Or maimed the merry throwers :
Or if they killed, those wingèd darts,
They killed but unprotected hearts ;
For flowers from flower-like hands can slay·
　　Jeanne Ray ! Jeanne Ray !

II.

Like humming-birds upon the breeze
　　So swiftly shot the posies ;
Glory of red anemones,
　　Pink buds of curled-up roses,

Lilacs and lilies of the vale ;
Yea, every flower that scents the gale
Yielded up incense to its day,
    Jeanne Ray ! Jeanne Ray !

III.

How gallantly along the course,
   Stepping with conscious glances,
Each flower-decked, gaily harnessed horse,
   In rank and file advances !
Even as green boughs and daisy-chains
Enwreathe their bits and bridle-reins,
Bright pleasure hides black grief away
    Jeanne Ray ! Jeanne Ray !

IV.

The people humming like a hive,
   Swarm closely pressed together,
To watch high fashion's crowded drive
   With flirt of fan and feather ;

And nosegays thrown up high in air,
Now hitting gray, now golden hair,
Now deftly caught upon their way,
  Jeanne Ray! Jeanne Ray!

V.

And past the eager jostling crowd,
  Watching their guests from far lands,
Gigs flash by in a violet cloud,
  And drags with rose-red garlands ;
There meet crowned heads from many zones,
And princes who have lost their thrones,
With gifts from Ind and far Cathay,
  Jeanne Ray! Jeanne Ray!

VI.

Ah, who shall bear away the prize
  In this bewitching battle,
Where shafts are hurled from brightest eyes,
  And Cupid's arrows rattle ;

In that fair fight where flowers alone
By fairer flowers are overthrown ?
Who shall be victor in this fray ?
    Jeanne Ray ! Jeanne Ray !

VII.

And people bet with buzz of tongue
  As the gay pageant passes ;
Now runs a murmur through the throng
  And stirs the thrilling masses.
All heads are turned, all necks astrain,
As through the thickening floral rain,
" Look ! look ! She comes !" you hear them say—
    Jeanne Ray ! Jeanne Ray !

VIII.

No turn-out in that festive throng
  Is half so bright and airy ;
Your cream-white ponies prance along
  As if they drew a fairy ;

They step along with heads held high,
And favours blue to match the sky:
They know theirs is the winning way,
    Jeanne Ray! Jeanne Ray!

IX.

\ queen in exile might you be,
    Or leader of the fashion?
Some Jenny Lind from over sea
    Melting all hearts with passion?
Some tragic Muse whose mighty spell
Unlocks the gates of heaven and hell?
What sceptre is it that you sway?
    Jeanne Ray! Jeanne Ray!

X.

All by yourself in spotless white,
    You sit there in your glory;
Your black eyes scintillate with light—
    Eyes that may hide a story.

In spotless white with ribbons blue,
You look fresh from a bath of dew
That sparkles in the rising day,
    Jeanne Ray! Jeanne Ray!

XI.

Triumphant—without shame or fear—
    You air a thousand graces;
Though women turn when you appear
    With cold, averted faces;
Though men at sight of you will stop,
As if they looked into a shop;
Shall both for this not doubly pay?
    Jeanne Ray! Jeanne Ray!

XII.

And with a smile upon your lips,
    Perhaps a shade too rosy,
You shake two dainty finger-tips
    And lightly fling a posy:

F

So might a high-born dame perchance,
In days of tourneys and romance,
Have flung her glove into the fray,
    Jeanne Ray! Jeanne Ray!

XIII.

As with that little careless sign
    You fling your bouquet lightly,
Three graybeards, flushing as with wine,
    Lift hats and bow politely;
And one, the grandest of the three,
Stoops low with stiff, rheumatic knee;
Out of the dust he picks your spray,
    Jeanne Ray! Jeanne Ray!

XIV.

His coat is all ablaze with stars
    For deeds of martial daring;
His name, a watchword in the wars,
    Kept soldiers from despairing.

Now see beside his orders rare
Your mignonette and maidenhair ;
With just a nod you turn away,
    Jeanne Ray ! Jeanne Ray !

XV.

You turn to meet the wintry face
    Of an old beggar-woman,
Just there beyond the railed-in space,
    Brown, bony, hardly human ;
Who in her tatters seems at least
The skeleton of Egypt's feast ;
A ghastly emblem of decay,
    Jeanne Ray ! Jeanne Ray !

XVI.

With palsied head and shaking hand,
    As if it were December,
Grim by the barrier see her stand,
    Just mumbling a " Remember !

Remember in thy days of lust,
That fairest flesh must come to dust ;
Then have some pity while you may,"
   Jeanne Ray! Jeanne Ray!

XVII.

Why do you shiver at her glance,
   As if the wind blew chilly ?
Why does your rosy countenance
   Turn pale as any lily ?
The sun is warm, the sky is bright,
The sea dissolving into light
Breaks into blossom-bells of spray ;
   Jeanne Ray! Jeanne Ray!

XVIII.

Ah, could some instinct in your breast
   Reveal that beggar's story,
Would not your gay life lose its zest,
   Your empire lose its glory ?

Or would you only care to waste
Life's bounty in yet hotter haste?
For is the world not beauty's prey?
  Jeanne Ray! Jeanne Ray!

XIX.

Alighting at the beggar's feet,
  A bright Napoleon flashes!
Then gaily through the dust and heat
  Your light Victoria dashes.
Again your face is rosy clear,
As with a loud and ringing cheer
They hail you winner of the day,
  Jeanne Ray! Jeanne Ray!

XX.

And gloriously at set of sun,
  In triumph now departing,
The golden prize your flowers have won
  Leaves rival bosoms smarting.

How many deem you half divine,
Where amid bouquets you recline—
Proud beauty in the devil's pay,
     Jeanne Ray ! Jeanne Ray !

XXI.

Down, down beneath the rolling wheels,
     The flowers, so fresh this morning,
Lie trampled under careless heels,
     Vile stuff for all men's scorning.
The roses crushed, the lilies soiled,
The violets of their sweets despoiled,
In dusty heaps defile your way,
     Jeanne Ray ! Jeanne Ray !

THE SONG OF THE WILLI.

According to a widespread Hungarian superstition—showing the ingrained national passion for dancing—the Willi or Willis were the spirits of young affianced girls who, dying before marriage, could not rest in their graves. It was popularly believed that these phantoms would nightly haunt lonely heaths in the neighbourhood of their native villages till the disconsolate lovers came as if drawn by a magnetic charm. On their appearance the Willi would dance with them without intermission till they dropped dead from exhaustion.

I.

THE wild wind is whistling o'er moorland and
    heather,
        Heigh-ho, heigh-ho!
I rise from my bed, and my bed has no feather,
        Heigh-ho!
My bed is deep down in the brown sullen mould,
  My head is laid low on the clod ;
So wormy the sheets, and the pillow so cold,
  Of clammy and moist clinging sod.

II.

The lone livid moon rides alone high in heaven,

      Heigh-ho, heigh-ho!

The stars' cutting glitter their dull shrouds hath

    riven,

      Heigh-ho!

I rise and I glide out far into the night,

    A shadow so swift and so still;

Bleak, bleak is the moonshine all ghastly and

    white,

    The dank morass drinketh its fill.

III.

And down in yon valley in wan vapour shrinking,

      Heigh-ho, heigh-ho!

The bare moated town cowers fitfully blinking,

      Heigh-ho!

There, warm under shelter, the fire burning bright,

    My lover sleeps sound in his bed;

But I flit alone in the pitiless night,
  Unpitied, unloved, and unwed.

IV.

And hast thou forgotten the deep troth we
    plighted ?
              Heigh-ho, heigh-ho !
Too warm was thy love by cold death to be
    blighted,
              Heigh-ho !
My sweetheart ! and mind'st thou that this is the
    night,
  The night that we should have been wed ?
And while I flit restless, a low wailing sprite,
  Ah, say, canst thou sleep in thy bed ?

V.

A week, but a week, and a wreath of gay
    flowers,
              Heigh-ho, heigh-ho !

I wore as I vied with the fleet-footed hours,

        Heigh-ho!

As I vied with the hours in dancing them down

    Till the stars reeled low in the sky,

And sweet came thy whispers as rose-leaves when

      blown

    About in the breeze of July.

        VI.

" Thou'rt light, O my chosen; a bird is not

      lighter,

        O love, my love!

I'd dance into death with thee; death would be

      brighter,

        My love!"

And they struck up a wild and a wonderful

      measure;

    Quick, quick beat our hearts to the tune;

Quick, quick the feet flew in a frenzy of pleasure,

    To the sound of the fife and bassoon.

VII.

On, on whirled the pairs on the swift music driven,
      Heigh-ho, heigh-ho!
Like gossamer vapours afloat in high heaven,
      Heigh-ho!
Like gossamer vapours, in silence they fled,
   With a shifting of face into face;
But fleeter than all the fleet dancers we sped
   In the rush of the rapturous race.

VIII.

How often turned Wanda, the slim, lily-throated,
      Heigh-ho, heigh-ho!
And gazed at us wistful as onward we floated,
      Heigh-ho!
And Bilba, the swarthy, whose eyes had the trick
   Of a stag's, with a glitter of steel;
She lifted her lashes, so long and so thick,
   To stare at my true love and leal.

IX.

But he, he saw none o' them, brown-faced or rosy,

      Heigh-ho, heigh-ho!

Tho' maidens bloomed bright like a fresh-gathered

  posy,

      Heigh-ho!

For his eyes that shone black as the sloes of the

  hedges,

  They shone like two stars over me ;

And his breath, thrilling o'er me as wind over

  sedges,

  Stirred my hair till I tingled with glee.

X.

Now slow as two down-bosomed swans, we were

  sliding,

      Heigh-ho, heigh-ho!

O'er the low heaving swell of the silver sounds

  gliding,

      Heigh-ho!

Now hollowly booming drums rumbled apace,

    Flashed sharp clatt'ring cymbals around,

And swung like loose leaves in a stormy embrace

    We whirled in a tumult of sound.

XI.

But pallid our cheeks grew, late flushing with

      pleasure,

        Heigh-ho, heigh-ho!

As slowly away swooned the languishing measure,

        Heigh-ho!

For shrill crew the cock as the sun 'gan to rise,

    And it rang from afar like a knell ;

Our kisses grew bitter and sweet grew our sighs,

    As sadly we murmured, " Farewell ! "

XII.

High up in the chambers the maidens together,

        O love, my love!

Were piling bleached linen as white as swan's
    feather
        My love!
Were weaving and spinning and singing aloud,
    While broidering my bride-veil of lace ;
But the three fatal sisters they wove me my
    shroud,
    And death kissed me cold on the face.

XIII.

The wild wind is whistling o'er moorland and
    heather,
        Heigh-ho, heigh-ho!
I rise from my bed, and my bed has no feather,
        Heigh-ho!
The snow driveth grisly and ghostly, and gleams
    In the glare of the moon's chilly glance ;
What pale flitting phantoms aroused by her beams,
    Are circling in shadowy dance!

XIV.

Mayhap ye were maidens death plucked in your
    flower,
          Heigh-ho, heigh-ho!
As clustering you glowed in love's murmuring
    bower,
          Heigh-ho!
Who, delirious for life from the gloom of your
    graves,
    Are driven to wander with me,
And you rise from your tombs like the white-
    crested waves
    From the depths of the dolorous sea.

XV.

Ah, maidens, pale maidens, o'er moorland and
    heather,
          Heigh-ho, heigh-ho!
The bridegroom is coming athwart the wild
    weather,
          Heigh-ho!

Full shines the fair moon on his beautiful face,
  He walketh like one in a trance ;
Nay, is running like one who is running a race
  Against death, with his dead bride to dance.

XVI.

At the sound of thy footfall my numb heart is
    shaken,
        O love, my love !
Once again all its pulses to new life awaken,
        My love !
It leaps like a stag that is borne as on wings
  To the brooks thawing thick through the noon,
Like a lark from the glebe, like a lily that springs
  From its bier to the bosom of June.

XVII.

" I hold thee, I hold thee, I drink thy caresses,
        O love, my love ! "

Round thy face, round thy throat, I roll my dank
 tresses,
    My love!
" I hold thee, I hold thee! Eight nights, wan and
 weeping,"
 I wandered loud sobbing thy name!
" Thy lips are as cold as the snowdrift a-sweeping ; "
 But thy breath soon shall fan them to flame!

XVIII.

Blow up for the dance now o'er moorland and
 heather!
   Heigh-ho, heigh-ho!
Blow, blow you wild winds, while we two dance
 together,
   Heigh-ho!
Till the clouds dance above with tempestuous
 embraces
 Of maidenly moonbeams in flight ;
In the silvery rear of whose fugitive traces
 Reel the stars through the revelling night!

       G

XIX.

" Cocks crow, and the breath on thy sweet lip is
　failing,

　　　O love, my love ! "

Stars swoon, and the flame in thy dark eye is
　quailing,

　　　My love !

" Oh, brighter the night than the fires of the day "

　When thine eyes shine as stars over me !

" Oh, sweeter thy grave than the soft breath of
　May ! "

　Then down, Love, to death, but with thee.

SCHERZO.

Oh, beloved, come and bring
All the flowery wealth of spring !
Though the leaf be in the sere,
Icy winter creeping near ;
Though the trees like mourners all
Standing at a funeral,
Black against the pallid air
Toss their wild arms in despair,
With their bald heads sadly bowed
O'er dead summer in her shroud.
Yea, though golden days be o'er,
If you enter at my door,
Spring, dear spring, will come once more.
There will break upon the night

That glad flash of dewy light
Which, like young love in a pet,
Once with sunny tears would wet
Many a wild-wood violet ;
And the hyacinth will arise
In the April of your eyes.
Blossoms of the apple tree?
Rarer blossoms bloom for me
In the cunning white and red,
Most felicitously wed,
On your cheek.   And then your brow—
Can a snow-white cherry-bough
Match its bland, unsullied hue,
Where, like threads of silky blue,
Little veins show here and there
Through broad temples where your hair,
Clustering, hangs a tender brown
Softer than the fluffy down
Which before the leaf in March
Beards the lime tree and the larch?

Shall I grieve because the rose,

The red rose, no longer blows,

Since all roses you eclipse

With the roses of your lips?

And what matter, O my sweet,

Though the genial light and heat

Have departed for a while!

Only let me see you smile,

Let me see that dulcet curve

Like a dimpling wavelet swerve

Round the coral of your mouth,

And the North will change to South:

To the happy South, whose clear

Light o'er-brimming atmosphere,

Flowing in at every pore,

Sets life glowing to the core.

You are light and life in sooth,

Fair as was that Grecian youth

Who in her cold sphere above

Drove poor Dian mad with love—

When she saw him where he lay,

White and golden like a spray

Of tall jonquils whose intense

Sweetness faints upon the sense ;

When she saw him swathed in light,

Couched on the aërial height

Of hoar Latmos, hushed and warm ;

While, to shield him from all harm,

Like a woman's rounded arm,

A fresh creeper wildly fair

Twined around his throat and hair.

And the goddess clean forgot

Her fair fame without a blot,

And untarnished reputation,

Free from faintest imputation

Of such frailties as the fair

Dwellers in Elysian air

Find recorded to their shame,

Chronicled with date and name,

In the annals of the skies.

She forgot in her surprise,
When her empyrean eyes
Saw Endymion where he lay
Slumbering, and she cast away
Her immortal honour, clear
As her own unclouded sphere,
For the palpitating bliss
Of a surreptitious kiss.

Oh, beloved, come and bring
All the flowery wealth of spring—
All its blossoms, buds, and bells,
And wind-coaxing violet smells—
All its miracle of grace
In the blossom of your face.

LYRICS.

LOVE'S SOMNAMBULIST.

LIKE some wild sleeper who alone at night
Walks with unseeing eyes along a height,
   With death below and only stars above ;
I, in broad daylight, walk as if in sleep,
Along the edges of life's perilous steep,
   The lost somnambulist of love.

I, in broad day, go walking in a dream,
Led on in safety by the starry gleam
   Of thy blue eyes that hold my heart in thrall ;
Let no one wake me rudely, lest one day,
Startled to find how far I've gone astray,
   I dash my life out in my fall.

A MEETING.

A TWILIGHT glow diffused on high
  Flushed all the autumn land beneath ;
Like love that lights your azure eye,
    The pond's blue goblet on the heath
      Was brimful of the sky.

We met by chance, and heaven's rich hue
  Leaped to your face in rosy flame ;
Ah, is it possible you knew
    The wild delight that filled my frame
      As I caught sight of you ?

Ah, is it possible, my love,

 That your delight can equal mine?

Nay, then, the burning sky above

 Grows pale beside this bliss divine,

  And the deep glow thereof.

YOUR FACE.

I TOOK your face into my dreams,
    It floated round me like a light ;
Your beauty's consecrating beams
    Lay mirrored in my heart all night.
As in a lonely mountain mere,
    Unvisited of any streams,
Supremely bright and still and clear,
    The solitary moonlight gleams,
    Your face was shining in my dreams.

ONLY A SMILE.

No butterfly whose frugal fare
   Is breath of heliotrope and clove,
And other trifles light as air,
   Could live on less than doth my love.

That childlike smile that comes and goes
   About your gracious lips and eyes,
Hath all the sweetness of the rose,
   Which feeds the freckled butterflies.

I feed my love on smiles, and yet
   Sometimes I ask, with tears of woe,
How had it been if we had met,
   If you had met me long ago,

Before the fast, defacing years
    Had made all ill that once was well?
Ah, then your smiling breeds such tears
    As Tantalus may weep in hell.

SOMETIMES I WONDER.

SOMETIMES I wonder if you guess
The deep impassioned tenderness
   Which overflows my heart ;
The love I never dare confess ;
Yet hard, yea, harder to repress
   Than tears too fain to start.

Sometimes I ponder, O my sweet,
The things I'll tell you when we meet ;
   But straightway at your sight
My heart's blood oozes to my feet
Like thawing waters in the heat,
   Confused with too much light.

II

I hardly know, when you are near,

If it is love, or joy, or fear

    Which fills my languid frame ;

Enveloped in your atmosphere,

My dark self seems to disappear,

    A moth entombed in flame.

MANY WILL LOVE YOU.

MANY will love you; you were made for love;
For the soft plumage of the unruffled dove
  Is not so soft as your caressing eyes.
You will love many; for the winds that veer
Are not more prone to shift their compass, dear,
  Than your quick fancy flies.

Many will love you; but I may not, no;
Even though your smile sets all my life aglow,
  And at your fairness all my senses ache.
You will love many; but not me, my dear,
Who have no gift to give you but a tear
  Sweet for your sweetness' sake.

A DREAM.

ONLY a dream, a beautiful baseless dream ;
Only a bright
Flash from your eyes, a brief electrical gleam,
Charged with delight.

Only a waking, alone, in the moon's last gleam
Fading from sight ;
Only a flooding of tears that shudder and stream
Fast through the night.

ROSE D'AMOUR.

I PLANTED a rose tree in my garden,
  In early days when the year was young ;
I thought it would bear me roses, roses,
  While nights were dewy and days were long.

It bore but once, and a white rose only—
  A lovely rose with petals of light ;
Like the moon in heaven, supreme and lonely ;
  And the lightning struck it one summer night.

SONNET.

EVEN as on some black background full of night,
   And hollow storm in cloudy disarray,
   The forceful brush of some great master may
More brilliantly evoke a higher light ;
So beautiful, so delicately white,
   So like a very metaphor of May,
   Your loveliness on my life's sombre gray
In its perfection stands out doubly bright.

And yet your beauty breeds a strange despair,
   And pang of yearning in the helpless heart,
To shield you from time's fraying wear and tear
   That from yourself yourself would wrench apart ;
How save you, fairest, but to set you where
   Mortality kills death in deathless art ?

A PARTING.

THE year is on the wing, my love,
    With tearful days and nights ;
The clouds are on the wing above
    With gathering swallow-flights.

The year is on the wing, my sweet,
    And in the ghostly race,
With patter of unnumbered feet,
    The dead leaves fly apace.

The year is on the wing, and shakes
    The last rose from its tree ;
And I, whose heart in parting breaks,
    Must bid adieu to thee.

MY LADY.

LIKE putting forth upon a sea
  On which the moonbeams shimmer,
Where reefs and unknown perils be
To wreck, yea, wreck one utterly,
It were to love you, lady fair,
In whose black braids of billowy hair
  The misty moonstones glimmer.

Oh, misty moonstone-coloured eyes,
  Latticed behind long lashes,
Within whose clouded orbs there lies,
Like lightning in the sleeping skies,

A spark to kindle and ignite,

And set a fire of love alight

    To burn one's heart to ashes.

I will not put forth on this deep

    Of perilous emotion ;

No, though your hands be soft as sleep,

They shall not have my heart to keep,

Nor draw it to your fatal sphere.

Lady, you are as much to fear

    As is the fickle ocean.

ON A VIOLA D'AMORE.

CARVED WITH A CUPID'S HEAD, AND PLAYED ON
FOR THE FIRST TIME AFTER MORE THAN A
CENTURY.

WHAT fairy music clear and light,
 Responsive to your fingers,
Swells rippling on the summer night,
 And amorously lingers
Upon the sense, as long ago
In days of rouge and rococo!

A century of silence lay
 On strings that had not spoken
Since powdered lords to ladies gay
 Gave, for a lover's token,

Fans glowing fresh from Watteau's art,
Well worth a marchioness's heart.

Your dormant music tranced and bound
   Was like the Sleeping Beauty
Prince Charming in the forest found,
   And kissed in loyal duty :
And when she woke her eyes' blue fire
Turned the dumb forest to a lyre.

Thus Amor with the bandaged eyes,
   Fit symbol of hushed numbers,
Most musically wakes and sighs
   After an age of slumbers :
Beneath your magic bow's control
The Viol has regained her soul.

A CHILD'S FANCY.

"Hush, hush! Speak softly, Mother dear,
So that the daisies may not hear;
For when the stars begin to peep,
The pretty daisies go to sleep.

"See, Mother, round us on the lawn;
With soft white lashes closely drawn,
They've shut their eyes so golden-gay,
That looked up through the long, long day.

"But now they're tired of all the fun—
Of bees and birds, of wind and sun
Playing their game at hide-and-seek ;—
Then very softly let us speak."

A myriad stars above the child
Looked down from heaven and sweetly smiled ;
But not a star in all the skies
Beamed on him with his Mother's eyes.

She stroked his curly chestnut head,
And whispering very softly, said,
" I'd quite forgotten they might hear ;
Thank you for that reminder, dear."

LASSITUDE.

I LAID me down beside the sea,
Endless in blue monotony ;
The clouds were anchored in the sky,
Sometimes a sail went idling by.

Upon the shingles on the beach
Gray linen was spread out to bleach,
And gently with a gentle swell
The languid ripples rose and fell.

A fisher-boy, in level line,
Cast stone by stone into the brine :
Methought I too might do as he,
And cast my sorrows on the sea.

The old, old sorrows in a heap
Dropped heavily into the deep ;
But with its sorrow on that day
My heart itself was cast away.

SEEKING.

IN many a shape and fleeting apparition,
    Sublime in age or with clear morning eyes,
Ever I seek thee, tantalizing Vision,
        Which beckoning flies.

Ever I seek Thee, O evasive Presence,
    Which on the far horizon's utmost verge,
Like some wild star in luminous evanescence,
        Shoots o'er the surge.

Ever I seek Thy features ever flying,
    Which ne'er beheld I never can forget :
Lightning which flames through love, and mimics
        dying
            In souls that set.

Ever I seek Thee through all clouds of error ;
   As when the moon behind earth's shadow slips,
She wears a momentary mask of terror
      In brief eclipse.

Ever I seek Thee, passionately yearning ;
   Like altar-fire on some forgotten fane,
My life flames up irrevocably burning,
      And burnt in vain.

THE END.

PRINTED BY WILLIAM CLOWES AND SONS, LIMITED,
LONDON AND BECCLES.

WORKS BY MATHILDE BLIND.

Poetry.

THE PROPHECY OF SAINT ORAN, and other Poems.

THE HEATHER ON FIRE.

THE ASCENT OF MAN.

Prose Fiction.

TARANTELLA : A Romance.

Monographs.

GEORGE ELIOT.

MADAME ROLAND

PRINTED BY WILLIAM CLOWES AND SONS, LIMITED,
LONDON AND BECCLES.

WORKS BY MATHILDE BLIND.

Poetry.

THE PROPHECY OF SAINT ORAN, and other Poems.

THE HEATHER ON FIRE.

THE ASCENT OF MAN.

Prose Fiction.

TARANTELLA : A Romance.

Monographs.

GEORGE ELIOT.

MADAME ROLAND

THE PROPHECY OF SAINT ORAN,

And other Poems.

"There is perhaps no phase of our history more capable of poetic treatment than the sainted lives of the Irish monks who first spread the Christian faith over the western shores of Scotland, and yet it would be difficult to point to a single representative poem having Saint Columba and the devoted band of his disciples for its heroes. An attempt at filling up this gap has recently been made by Miss Blind in a narrative poem devoted to the fate of St. Oran, the friend and disciple of St. Columba. . . . Apart from the sonorous beauty of her lines, there is in her diction a straightforwardness and simplicity, and an entire absence of affectation and false sentiment, which, combined with considerable power of characterization, make her volume a remarkable contribution to English literature."—*Times*, September 26, 1881.

"To disturb the *motif* of a legend is always a bold, and mostly a rash, proceeding. . . . And yet so skilfully is the story handled that the main incidents of the legend do not lose, but gain by this disturbance of the *motif*, and the character of Oran, which with the old *motif* could only have presented the single side of the religious enthusiast, becomes a character exhibiting that complexity which modern taste demands. . . . Directness of style and lucidity of narrative are the characteristic excellences of the poem. There are few contemporary poets who could have done so much dramatic business in so few lines. . . . In each of the sonnets there is a thought that is well expressed, and worth expressing."—*Athenæum*, July 30, 1881.

"It is in the domain of character that the poem is distinguished by its highest excellence. There is an ideal statuesqueness embodied in the person of St. Columba such as is felt to possess a powerful appeal to the imagination. The poem embraces many passions, of which the most tender and beautiful finds expression in the exquisite creation of the radiant golden-haired girl for whose love St. Oran breaks his vow of chastity. But the really powerful contribution to our knowledge of character which this book contains is fittingly centred in St. Oran himself. A dramatic instinct of high order finds utterance in his struggles between opposing passions. Nor are the metrical excellences of the poem less conspicuous. . . . If one were in need of some single phrase by which to denote the ultimate effect produced by this book, one might say that it seems the most *mature* of all recent first efforts, even of established rank."—*Academy*, July 16, 1881.

"In the choice of a subject for her chief poem she has been singularly fortunate. . . . That a story such as this is full of poetical suggestiveness is obvious, and Miss Blind has proved herself equal to the occasion. She has avoided writing anything approaching to a 'tendency poem.' She metes out justice with an equal hand to all her characters. The genuine enthusiasm and religious zeal of the monks are set forth in language as inspired as is the final protest of St. Oran against their narrow fanaticism; and one of the best passages in the book is indeed the Sermon in which St. Columba announces the Gospel of love and redemption to the islanders."—*Pall Mall Gazette*, August 22, 1881.

" ' The Prophecy of Saint Oran ' is skilfully told and vigorously written. In the description of nature and scenery; in the delineation of character ; and in the management of singularly difficult positions there is visible a firm and practised hand, a bold and unmistakable power. 'The Street Children's Dance' not unworthily ranks with some of the touching pieces of Hood, Mrs. Barrett Browning, and others."—*British Mail*, September 1, 1881.

" The only excuse for street music that can reasonably be considered valid is the touching plea for public toleration which is embodied in Miss Mathilde Blind's poem, wherein the spectacle of poor children dancing round an organ is as pathetically moralized and as tender and full of loving pity as Mrs. Browning's 'Cry of the Children.'"—*Daily Telegraph*, September 1, 1881.

" The poem is rich in true description of sea and sky and mountain, and glows in sympathy with the deeper feelings which stir humanity. There has been published no poem of such creative suggestiveness as this for many a day, and we hope and believe that it is the precursor of other work by the same unfaltering hand ! This poem is a true work of art, complete and beautiful. There is in the volume other work which shows a master's touch. . . ."—*Manchester Examiner and Times*, July 1, 1882.

" Il y a là bien plus qu'une simple facilité de versification. Le récit du poeme d'ouverture est grand et fort, la manière de raconter est pleine de poésie et d'effet Depuis la mort de Mrs. Barrett Browning, nous n'avons point eu de poésie aussi hautement inspirée qui ait jailli d'une source féminine."—*Le Livre*, Paris, October 10, 1881.

THE HEATHER ON FIRE:

A Tale of the Highland Clearances.

" Miss Blind has produced one of the most noticeable and moving poems which recent years have added to our shelves. . . . As a singer with a message her attempt is praiseworthy, and her performance is fairly self-consistent. It is eminently homogeneous ; the passion once felt, the inspiration once obeyed, the well-head pours forth its stream in a strong and uniform current, which knows no pause until its impulse ceases. . . . The story is pathetic at once in its simplicity and in its terror. . . . We congratulate the author upon her boldness in choosing a subject of our own time, fertile in what is pathetic, and free from any taint of the vulgar and conventional. Poetry of late years has tended too much towards motives of a merely fanciful and abstruse, sometimes a plainly artificial, character ; and we have had much of lyrical energy or attraction, with little of the real marrow of human life, the flesh and blood of man and woman. Positive subject-matter, the emotion which inheres in actual life, the very smile and the very tear and heart-pang, are, after all, precious to poetry, and we have them here. 'The Heather on Fire' may possibly prove to be something of a new departure, and one that was certainly not superfluous."—*Athenæum*, July 17, 1886.

" Miss Blind has chosen for her new poem one of the se terrible Highland clearances which stain the history of Scotch landlordism. Though her tale is a fiction it is too well founded on fact. . . . It may be said generally of the poem that the most difficult scenes are those in which Miss Blind succeeds best ; and on the whole we are inclined to think that its greatest and most surprising success is the picture of the poor old soldier Rory driven mad by the burning of his wife. In his frenzy he mixes up his old battles with the French and the descent of the landlord's ejectors upon the village."—*Academy*, August 7, 1886.

"In this versified tale of Highland clearances, Mathilde Blind has, with genuine poetic instinct, selected a family the fortunes of which form the burden of her story. . . . Literature and poetry are never seen at their best save in contact with actual life. . . . This little book abounds in vivid delineation of character, and is redolent with the noblest human sympathy."—*Newcastle Daily Chronicle*, June 3, 1886.

"A subject which has painfully preoccupied public opinion is, in the poem entitled 'The Heather on Fire,' treated with characteristic power by Miss Mathilde Blind. Irish evictions have offered so convenient a theme to party strife, that the sufferings of the unhappy Highland crofters have not always met with the compassion they were so well calculated to inspire. In eloquent and forcible verse, Miss Blind tells the tale of their wrongs, their resistance to the hard fate imposed upon them, and describes the bitter grief with which

> 'Crowding on the decks with hungry eyes,
> Straining toward the coast that flies and flies,'

those among them driven into exile look on the shores to which many bid an eternal farewell. Both as a narrative and descriptive poem 'The Heather on Fire' is equally remarkable."—*Morning Post*, July 30, 1886.

"We are happy in being able to extend to the present poem a welcome equally sincere and equally hearty; for it is a poem that is rich not only in power and beauty but in that 'enthusiasm of humanity' which stirs and moves us, and of which so much contemporary verse is almost painfully deficient. Miss Blind does not possess her theme; she is possessed by it, as was Mrs. Browning when she wrote 'Aurora Leigh.' . . . We can best describe the kind of her success by noting the fact that while engaged in the perusal of her book we do not say, 'What a fine poem!' but 'What a terrible story!' or, more probably still, say nothing at all, but read on and on under the spell of a great horror and an overpowering pity. Poetry of which this can be said needs no other recommendation, and, therefore, we need not unduly lengthen our review of 'The Heather on Fire.'"—*Manchester Examiner and Times*, September 1, 1886.

"There are charming pictures of West Highland scenery, in Arran apparently, and of the surroundings and conditions of Highland cottar life."—*Scotsman*, July 20, 1886.

"In 'The Heather on Fire' she exhibits a clearness and beauty of diction, a rhythmical correctness, a grace and simplicity of style which mark her out as no slavish follower of any poetic 'school,' but an unaffected and truthful expression of her own feelings. . . . Whatever the reader's opinion may be on the grievance which Miss Blind throws into such fierce light, he cannot fail to be pleased with her graceful tale, so gracefully and simply told."—*Glasgow Herald*, July 20, 1886.

"Miss Mathilde Blind's poem is the tragic epic of the old evictions in the Highlands of Scotland. It is a strange fact that the general reader knows more about the siege of Troy, the Norman Conquest, and the Wars of the Roses, than about such matters in the very history of our own days as the depopulation of the Highlands of Scotland by the landlords. The old story comes to the front just now by reason of the crofter agitation. In the preface to her fine and touching epic, and in the notes at the end, Miss Blind passes in review some of the facts of the eviction of the Glen Sannox people by the Duke of Hamilton in 1832, where, as she says, 'the progress of civilization, which has redeemed many a wilderness and gladdened the solitary places of the world, has come with a curse to these Highland glens, and turned green pastures and golden harvest fields once more into a desert.' The 'Heather on Fire' is a poem in four cantos—or 'Duans'—comprising about two hundred stanzas."—*School Board Chronicle*, July 10, 1886.

"It is written in a strain which must of necessity appeal to the sympathies of all grades of society, and at the same time it is eminently poetical, both in thought and rhythm."—*Western Antiquary*, August, 1886.

"A book like this forms an admirable corrective to the harsh and cold-blooded theories of such landlords as the Duke of Argyle on the rights of his class."—*Cambridge Independent Press*, August, 1886.

"There is a sonorous beauty, a classic dignity and depth of pathos throughout her four cantos, and a vivid and thrilling description is given of the industrious hamlets, the contented happy people, and the ruthless manner in which the evictions were effected by the stewards and ground-officers."—*Elgin Courant*, August, 1886.

TARANTELLA:

A Romance.

"The author of this two-volumed romance is favourably known by other works, and by her appreciative 'Life of George Eliot.' The strange effects of the bite of a tarantula spider, so firmly believed in by the Italian peasantry, and the marvellous power of musical enthusiasm, supply the motive of the story; and the characters are portrayed with great force, pathos, and a touch of homely humour."—*Bookseller*, Christmas, 1884.

"Miss Blind may be congratulated on 'Tarantella,' her first novel. In the *récit* (as we have called it) of the musician, Emanuel Sturm, nearly all the interest of the book is concentrated. The violinist, poor and unknown, finds himself at Capri. Accident brings him, one evening, to a frightened group of women, one of whom has just been bitten by the tarantula, and, according to the popular superstition, he is implored to play, in order to drive the poison out of her. He refuses at first, but afterwards consents, and, finding himself almost supernaturally inspired, plays an improvised 'Tarantella' throughout a whole stormy night, finally curing the girl. The tune thus strangely hit on spreads, and ultimately makes him famous, but the love he has conceived for his Antonella brings him almost as much misery as his music brings him fame."—*Pall Mall Gazette*, February 5, 1885.

"Admiration of the delicate sketching now in vogue should not blind us to the very opposite kind of charm of which 'Tarantella' is full. Entirely poetical in conception (save that it is not written in metre), 'Tarantella' is more essentially a poem than many a narrative written in smooth and elegant verse. . . . 'Tarantella' is indeed full of strange originality and scenic effects of uncommon powers. The dance among the ruins is not likely to be soon forgotten by the most unimaginative of readers, and it is rarely, we think, that in an English novel the psychology of the poetic temperament has been touched by a hand so delicate and at the same time so strong."—*Athenæum*, January 17, 1885.

"There is abundant imagination, and the language is generally fresh and vigorous. . . . The author finds many opportunities of introducing scenes from German life, which are evidently written with intimate knowledge. . . . This is distinctly a novel to read."—*Echo*, June 16, 1886.

"This powerful and pathetic tale has carried us more completely out of ourselves and along with it than any work of fiction we have read for many a day. . . . Her (Miss Blind's) word pictures glow with rich local colours; she is a complete mistress of the art of dramatic cause and effect. When once fairly under weigh, she never allows the interest to flag for a single moment. Thus it is only when we have laid down the final volume that we have time or inclination to pause and recognize the care and art which have contributed to this triumphant result; to turn back . . . and dwell on the author's extraordinary knowledge of the human heart—extraordinary alike for its depth and its range. As for the wit and humour with which the book is freely sprinkled, the poetic and artistic spirit which pervades it thoughout, they can only be appreciated on a second or a third perusal."—*Life*, December 25, 1884.

"'Tarantella' is extremely clever, and the treatment of the weird subject she has chosen picturesque in the extreme. The local colouring is especially fine and her character studies extremely strong. Thrice welcome in its two-volume form, 'Tarantella' is a book bound to make its mark."—*Whitehall Review*, December 11, 1884.

"We have very ingenious resources in music and the bite of the tarantula, which alone music is said to heal. Notwithstanding the sense of improbability, we follow the strange fortunes of Antonella Countess Ogotshka, and her almost magical transformation with interest. Mina, the innocent girl, her friend, is well delineated, and Emanuel Sturm, the wonderful violinist and composer, for whose portrait Paganini has doubtless been available, is original, no less than his friend the painter."—*British Quarterly*, January, 1885.

"'Tarantella' is a very clever story, with plenty of action and not without tragic incidents. The author has also plenty of humour, and there is at least as much light as shade in the book. Mina is not less delightful than the Countess is objectionable, in spite of her beauty and her daring."—*London Figaro*, November 20, 1886.

"We shall not spoil the story by hinting at its *dénouement*. It is a deeply interesting one; and the characters, three of them at least, are sufficiently original to give the author a high rank as a novelist. . . . The book abounds in striking and interesting pictures of Italian and German life and scenery."—*Dublin Mail*, November, 1886.

"'Tarantella' is, indeed, a novel unlike the common—full of power and imagination and originality. . . . It would be unjust to deny to this very remarkable book a large share of what the world calls genius."—*Melbourne Argus*, March 14, 1885.

"By her recent works, 'The Prophecy of Saint Oran' and the 'Life of George Eliot,' Miss Blind brought herself before the public as a writer of considerable ability, and her latest novel will do much to increase her reputation. . . . 'Tarantella' deserves to be classed among the best novels of the present day."—*Scottish News*, June 15, 1886.

"There is an inherent charm about 'Tarantella' which will be apparent to the reader from a perusal of the first chapter. This agreeable quality does not end there, however. The whole of the tale, which is divided into forty-six chapters, is permeated with features of an exceptionaly attractive description. Not the least noteworthy character of the story is its novelty. Most of the incidents, which are carefully elaborated and follow in logical sequence, are conspicuous for an airy freshness in nature and treatment. Every chapter has its specific purpose, there being a uniform overflow of idea and sentiment; and each development of the pleasing romance opens to the mental vision of the thoughtful reader incidents of a more or less engrossing description. Continental scenes and customs are described with freeness and perspicuity, and the varied and eventful adventures of the principal characters—pleasingly typical, it may be mentioned, of the romanticism invariably associated with 'love's young dream,' when, as in the present instance, there is a combination of youth and beauty—are recorded with a poetical fervour and gracefulness of diction which are certain to be generally admired."—*Western Daily Press*, June 2, 1886.

THE ASCENT OF MAN:

Poems.

" Miss Blind traces the 'Ascent of Man' through successive stages, until first love, and then sorrow—which is love under another guise—lead us to the highest conception of human life we can hope to reach. It is a brave, sad, glorious story, told with inimitable skill, and as only a poet who knows man's heart, with its hopes, doubts, fears, aspirations, could possibly tell it. . . . The other poems in the volume are as excellent in their kind as those which give a title to it. The only difference between them is that one series is rich with human experience, and with the results of knowledge and of high thinking, while the other is all aglow with the fresh delights of the out-door world. These delights find an almost perfect expression. . . . A reviewer who is so fortunate as to light on a book like this, lays it down with regret, and fears that he has not said of it all that it deserves should be said. That is my feeling ; and, lest I should have omitted any note of praise that ought to be sounded, I should like to add, by way of suggestion to all lovers of poetry—and I hope they are still many—that here is truly a book that is worth the loving."—*Academy,* June 15, 1889.

"The effort which Miss Blind has made is one deserving of high praise. From Chaos to Kosmos she hurries her reader along, breathless and perspiring perhaps, but never anxious to stop. We have known her book to be read on the Underground Railway, and the reader to be so absorbed in its contents as to be carried unawares several stations past his destination. . . . Miss Blind's gift of song is genuine, and her imagination powerful. . . . When all is said and done, 'The Ascent of Man' remains a remarkable poem, and cannot fail to increase its author's reputation as a brilliant and original writer."—*Athenæum,* July 20, 1889.

" There is a fine elevation of tone, and there is a splendid mastery of diction, well sustained from the beginning to the end. . . . The poems are unquestionably very beautiful."—*School Board Chronicle,* June 8, 1889.

" Miss Blind has already a place of honour among poets, and this striking volume will make it sure. There is nothing weak or unreal about her verse, and there is much force of thought, sympathy for all, and burning scorn of luxurious vice."— *Liverpool Mercury,* June 19, 1889.

" One of the advanced minds of the day is Mathilde Blind. I have at my side her latest book, 'The Ascent of Man.' The poems are all earnest and high pitched in tone—they are human. . . . Every line comes from a heart full of life's unutterable woes, of hope's faint, half-believing monitions."—*Cheltenham Examiner,* June 19, 1889.

" To Miss Blind belongs the honour of having been the first to seriously render Charles Darwin and Herbert Spencer into verse on anything like a bold and comprehensive scale. 'The Ascent of Man' is a really remarkable poem. Its main conception is even noble, its manner of execution is brilliant and vigorous, and it abounds in passages which prove Miss Blind to possess the true poetic faculty."—*Wit and Wisdom,* August 3, 1889.

" In her last published volume of poems, 'The Ascent of Man,' Miss Blind has revealed qualities of imagination, enthusiasm, and strength, which place her high indeed among women writers of the day."—*Echo,* August 8, 1889.

"Miss Blind has already proved herself to be no ordinary writer of verse, and her new volume will add to her reputation. 'The Ascent of Man' is a philosophical poem, challenging comparison by its subject with the great work of Lucretius, and inevitably suggesting some of the finest passages of Tennyson."—*Manchester Examiner*, May 13, 1889.

"That Miss Blind's volume shows signs of poetic power no careful reader can for a moment doubt."—*Literary World*, June 14, 1889.

"Miss Blind is an accomplished authoress, and a verse-maker of remarkable skill. There is plenty of suggestion, as well as a good deal of brilliant, forcible, and easy colouring, in 'The Ascent of Man.'"—*Star*, June 17, 1889.

"This is a powerful but unequal poem : but the task set to herself by the author was such a mighty one, that, even had her success been far less than it is, she might well be proud. . . . This volume will considerably enhance Miss Blind's reputation as a poetess."—*Lady's Pictorial*, June 28, 1889.

"There are some fine passages, elevated in conception and felicitous in expression. . . . The volume, as a whole, is a considerable advance on Miss Blind's previous poetic work, and should give much pleasure to all thoughtful and cultivated readers."—*Globe*, May 22, 1889.

"The chief merit of this fine poem is that it treats from the transcendental point of view certain conceptions and theories of life which modern science has shown us under another aspect."—*St. James's Gazette*, June 19, 1889.

"'The Ascent of Man' is a volume of verse which is marked by much grace of diction. In her 'Poems of the Open Air,' Miss Blind is specially successful. Though a thousand poets have taken us into the gardens and fields ere now, we gladly return to them with her."—*British Weekly*, July 12, 1889.

"Her descriptions of the early struggles for existence are powerful and picturesque in a high degree."—*Pall Mall Gazette.*

"Has merit of no common order, due, perhaps, as much to the author's wide human sympathy as to her poetical gifts."—*Morning Post.*

"The doctrines and tendencies of present-day thought are endowed with fascinating poetic form in Miss Mathilde Blind's 'Ascent of Man.' . . . She encircles grave Science with an aureole, and illuminates his grey technical pages with rainbow tints and emblazoned designs."—*Watts's Literary Guide.*

"This new volume is another testimony to the sterling character of Miss Blind's poetic talent. Technically the verse-workmanship is masterly ; the verse is sonorous and well balanced, the diction simple and unaffected, and the style marked by the essential quality of distinction."—*Women's Penny Paper.*

"'The Ascent of Man' opens with lines which, in their vigour and rhythmic sweep, recall the most resonant passages of Lucretius."—*The Scottish Leader.*

𝕬 𝕷ist of 𝕭ooks

PUBLISHED BY

CHATTO & WINDUS,

214, Piccadilly, London, W.

Sold by all Booksellers, or sent post-free for the published price by the Publishers.

ABOUT.—THE FELLAH: An Egyptian Novel. By EDMOND ABOUT. Translated by Sir RANDAL ROBERTS. Post 8vo, illustrated boards, **2s.**

ADAMS (W. DAVENPORT), WORKS BY.
A DICTIONARY OF THE DRAMA. Being a comprehensive Guide to the Plays, Playwrights, Players, and Playhouses of the United Kingdom and America. Crown 8vo, half-bound. **12s. 6d.** [*Preparing.*
QUIPS AND QUIDDITIES. Selected by W. D. ADAMS. Post 8vo, cloth limp, **2s. 6d.**

ADAMS (W. H. D.).—WITCH, WARLOCK, AND MAGICIAN: Historical Sketches of Magic and Witchcraft in England and Scotland. By W. H. DAVENPORT ADAMS. Demy 8vo, cloth extra, **12s.**

AGONY COLUMN (THE) OF "THE TIMES," from 1800 to 1870. Edited, with an Introduction, by ALICE CLAY. Post 8vo, cloth limp, **2s. 6d.**

AIDE (HAMILTON), WORKS BY. Post 8vo, illustrated boards, **2s.** each.
CARR OF CARRLYON. | CONFIDENCES.

ALBERT.—BROOKE FINCHLEY'S DAUGHTER. By MARY ALBERT. Post 8vo, picture boards, **2s.**; cloth limp, **2s. 6d.**

ALEXANDER (MRS.), NOVELS BY. Post 8vo, illustrated boards, **2s.** each.
MAID, WIFE, OR WIDOW? | VALERIE'S FATE.

ALLEN (GRANT), WORKS BY. Crown 8vo, cloth extra, **6s.** each.
THE EVOLUTIONIST AT LARGE. | COLIN CLOUT'S CALENDAR.
Crown 8vo, cloth extra, **6s.** each; post 8vo, illustrated boards., **2s.** each,
STRANGE STORIES. With a Frontispiece by GEORGE DU MAURIER.
THE BECKONING HAND. With a Frontispiece by TOWNLEY GREEN.
Crown 8vo, cloth extra, **3s. 6d.** each; post 8vo, illustrated boards, **2s.** each.
PHILISTIA. | FOR MAIMIE'S SAKE. | THIS MORTAL COIL.
BABYLON. | IN ALL SHADES. | THE TENTS OF SHEM.
| THE DEVIL'S DIE. |
THE GREAT TABOO. Crown 8vo, cloth extra, **3s. 6d.**
DUMARESQ'S DAUGHTER. Three Vols., crown 8vo.

AMERICAN LITERATURE, A LIBRARY OF, from the Earliest Settlement to the Present Time. Compiled and Edited by EDMUND CLARENCE STEDMAN and ELLEN MACKAY HUTCHINSON. Eleven Vols., royal 8vo, cloth extra. A few copies are for sale by Messrs. CHATTO & WINDUS (published in New York by C. L. WEBSTER & Co.), price **£6 12s.** the set.

ARCHITECTURAL STYLES, A HANDBOOK OF. By A. ROSENGARTEN. Translated by W. COLLETT-SANDARS. With 639 Illusts. Cr. 8vo, cl. ex., **7s. 6d.**

ART (THE) OF AMUSING: A Collection of Graceful Arts, GAMES, Tricks, Puzzles, and Charades. By FRANK BELLEW. 300 Illusts. Cr. 8vo, cl. ex., **4s. 6d.**

ARNOLD (EDWIN LESTER), WORKS BY.
THE WONDERFUL ADVENTURES OF PHRA THE PHŒNICIAN. With Introduction by Sir EDWIN ARNOLD, and 12 Illusts. by H. M. PAGET. Cr. 8vo, cl., **3s. 6d.**
BIRD LIFE IN ENGLAND. Crown 8vo, cloth extra, **6s.**

ARTEMUS WARD'S WORKS: The Works of CHARLES FARRER BROWNE, better known as ARTEMUS WARD. With Portrait and Facsimile. Crown 8vo, cloth extra, **7s. 6d.**—Also a POPULAR EDITION, post 8vo, picture boards, **2s.**
THE GENIAL SHOWMAN: Life and Adventures of ARTEMUS WARD. By EDWARD P. HINGSTON. With a Frontispiece. Crown 8vo, cloth extra. **3s. 6d.**

ASHTON (JOHN), WORKS BY. Crown 8vo, cloth extra, **7s. 6d.** each.
HISTORY OF THE CHAP-BOOKS OF THE 18th CENTURY. With 334 Illusts.
SOCIAL LIFE IN THE REIGN OF QUEEN ANNE. With 85 Illustrations.
HUMOUR, WIT, AND SATIRE OF SEVENTEENTH CENTURY. With 82 Illusts.
ENGLISH CARICATURE AND SATIRE ON NAPOLEON THE FIRST. 115 Illusts.
MODERN STREET BALLADS. With 57 Illustrations.

BACTERIA.—A SYNOPSIS OF THE BACTERIA AND YEAST FUNGI AND ALLIED SPECIES. By W. B. GROVE, B.A. With 87 Illustrations. Crown 8vo, cloth extra, **3s. 6d.**

BARDSLEY (REV. C. W.), WORKS BY.
ENGLISH SURNAMES: Their Sources and Significations. Cr 8vo, cloth, **7s. 6d.**
CURIOSITIES OF PURITAN NOMENCLATURE. Crown 8vo, cloth extra, **6s.**

BARING GOULD (S., Author of "John Herring," &c.), NOVELS BY.
Crown 8vo, cloth extra, **3s. 6d.** each; post 8vo, illustrated boards, **2s.** each.
RED SPIDER. | EVE.

BARRETT (FRANK, Author of "Lady Biddy Fane,") NOVELS BY.
Post 8vo, illustrated boards, **2s.** each; cloth, **2s. 6d.** each.
FETTERED FOR LIFE. | BETWEEN LIFE AND DEATH.
THE SIN OF OLGA ZASSOULICH. Three Vols., crown 8vo.

BEACONSFIELD, LORD: A Biography. By T. P. O'CONNOR, M.P. Sixth Edition, with an Introduction. Crown 8vo, cloth extra, **5s.**

BEAUCHAMP.—GRANTLEY GRANGE: A Novel. By SHELSLEY BEAUCHAMP. Post 8vo, illustrated boards, **2s.**

BEAUTIFUL PICTURES BY BRITISH ARTISTS: A Gathering of Favourites from our Picture Galleries, beautifully engraved on Steel. With Notices of the Artists by SYDNEY ARMYTAGE, M.A. Imperial 4to, cloth extra, gilt edges, **21s.**

BECHSTEIN.—AS PRETTY AS SEVEN, and other German Stories. Collected by LUDWIG BECHSTEIN. With Additional Tales by the Brothers GRIMM, and 98 Illustrations by RICHTER. Square 8vo, cloth extra, **6s. 6d.**; gilt edges, **7s. 6d.**

BEERBOHM.—WANDERINGS IN PATAGONIA; or, Life among the Ostrich Hunters. By JULIUS BEERBOHM. With Illusts. Cr. 8vo, cl. extra, **3s. 6d.**

BESANT (WALTER), NOVELS BY.
Cr. 8vo, cl. ex., **3s. 6d.** each; post 8vo, illust. bds., **2s.** each; cl. limp, **2s. 6d.** each.
ALL SORTS AND CONDITIONS OF MEN. With Illustrations by FRED. BARNARD.
THE CAPTAINS' ROOM, &c. With Frontispiece by E. J. WHEELER.
ALL IN A GARDEN FAIR. With 6 Illustrations by HARRY FURNISS.
DOROTHY FORSTER. With Frontispiece by CHARLES GREEN.
UNCLE JACK, and other Stories | CHILDREN OF GIBEON.
THE WORLD WENT VERY WELL THEN. With 12 Illustrations by A. FORESTIER.
HERR PAULUS: His Rise, his Greatness, and his Fall.
FOR FAITH AND FREEDOM. With Illustrations by A. FORESTIER and F. WADDY.
TO CALL HER MINE, &c. With 9 Illustrations by A. FORESTIER.
THE BELL OF ST. PAUL'S.
Crown 8vo, cloth extra, **3s. 6d.** each.
ARMOREL OF LYONESSE: A Romance of To-day. With 12 Illusts. by F. BARNARD.
THE HOLY ROSE, &c. With Frontispiece by F. BARNARD.
ST. KATHERINE'S BY THE TOWER. With 12 full-page Illustrations by C. GREEN. Three Vols., crown 8vo.
FIFTY YEARS AGO. With 137 Plates and Woodcuts. Demy 8vo, cloth extra, **16s.**
THE EULOGY OF RICHARD JEFFERIES. With Portrait. Cr. 8vo, cl. extra, **6s.**
THE ART OF FICTION. Demy 8vo, **1s.**
LONDON. With nearly 100 Illustrations. Demy 8vo, cloth extra, **18s.** [Preparing.

BESANT (WALTER) AND JAMES RICE, NOVELS BY.
Cr. 8vo, cl. ex., 3s. 6d. each ; post 8vo, illust. bds., 2s. each; cl. limp, 2s. 6d. each.

READY-MONEY MORTIBOY.	BY CELIA'S ARBOUR.
MY LITTLE GIRL.	THE CHAPLAIN OF THE FLEET.
WITH HARP AND CROWN.	THE SEAMY SIDE.
THIS SON OF VULCAN.	THE CASE OF MR. LUCRAFT, &c.
THE GOLDEN BUTTERFLY.	'TWAS IN TRAFALGAR'S BAY, &c.
THE MONKS OF THELEMA.	THE TEN YEARS' TENANT, &c.

. There is also a LIBRARY EDITION of the above Twelve Volumes, handsomely
set in new type, on a large crown 8vo page, and bound in cloth extra, 6s. each.

BENNETT (W. C., LL.D.), WORKS BY. Post 8vo, cloth limp, 2s. each.
A BALLAD HISTORY OF ENGLAND. | SONGS FOR SAILORS.

BEWICK (THOMAS) AND HIS PUPILS. By AUSTIN DOBSON. With
05 Illustrations. Square 8vo. cloth extra, 6s.

BLACKBURN'S (HENRY) ART HANDBOOKS.
ACADEMY NOTES, separate years, from 1875-1887, 1889, and 1890, each 1s.
ACADEMY NOTES, 1891. With Illustrations. 1s.
ACADEMY NOTES, 1875-79. Complete in One Vol., with 600 Illusts. Cloth limp, 6s.
ACADEMY NOTES, 1880-84. Complete in One Vol., with 700 Illusts. Cloth limp, 6s.
GROSVENOR NOTES, 1877. 6d.
GROSVENOR NOTES, separate years, from 1878 to 1890, each 1s.
GROSVENOR NOTES, Vol. I., 1877-82. With 300 Illusts. Demy 8vo, cloth limp, 6s.
GROSVENOR NOTES, Vol. II., 1883-87. With 300 Illusts. Demy 8vo, cloth limp, 6s.
THE NEW GALLERY, 1888-1890. With numerous Illustrations, each 1s.
THE NEW GALLERY, 1891. With Illustrations. 1s.
ENGLISH PICTURES AT THE NATIONAL GALLERY. 114 Illustrations. 1s.
OLD MASTERS AT THE NATIONAL GALLERY. 128 Illustrations. 1s. 6d.
ILLUSTRATED CATALOGUE TO THE NATIONAL GALLERY. 242 Illusts. cl., 3s.

THE PARIS SALON, 1891. With Facsimile Sketches. 3s.
THE PARIS SOCIETY OF FINE ARTS, 1891. With Sketches. 3s. 6d.

BLAKE (WILLIAM) : India-proof Etchings from his Works by WILLIAM
BELL SCOTT. With descriptive Text. Folio, half-bound boards. 21s.

BLIND (MATHILDE), Poems by. Crown 8vo, cloth extra, 5s. each.
THE ASCENT OF MAN.
DRAMAS IN MINIATURE. With a Frontispiece by FORD MADOX BROWN.

BOURNE (H. R. FOX), WORKS BY.
ENGLISH MERCHANTS: Memoirs in Illustration of the Progress of British Commerce. With numerous Illustrations. 7s. 6d.
ENGLISH NEWSPAPERS: The History of Journalism. Two Vols., demy 8vo, cl., 25s.
THE OTHER SIDE OF THE EMIN PASHA RELIEF EXPEDITION. Crown 8vo,
cloth extra, 6s.

BOWERS' (G.) HUNTING SKETCHES. Oblong 4to, hf.-bd. bds., 21s. each.
CANTERS IN CRAMPSHIRE. | LEAVES FROM A HUNTING JOURNAL.

BOYLE (FREDERICK), WORKS BY. Post 8vo, illustrated boards, 2s. each.
CHRONICLES OF NO-MAN'S LAND. | CAMP NOTES.
SAVAGE LIFE. Crown 8vo, cloth extra, 3s. 6d. ; post 8vo, picture boards, 2s.

BRAND'S OBSERVATIONS ON POPULAR ANTIQUITIES ; chiefly
illustrating the Origin of our Vulgar Customs, Ceremonies, and Superstitions. With
the Additions of Sir HENRY ELLIS, and Illustrations. Cr. 8vo, cloth extra, 7s. 6d.

BREWER (REV. DR.), WORKS BY.
THE READER'S HANDBOOK OF ALLUSIONS, REFERENCES, PLOTS, AND
STORIES. Fifteenth Thousand. Crown 8vo, cloth extra, 7s. 6d.
AUTHORS AND THEIR WORKS, WITH THE DATES: Being the Appendices to
"The Reader's Handbook," separately printed. Crown 8vo, cloth limp, 2s.
A DICTIONARY OF MIRACLES. Crown 8vo, cloth extra, 7s. 6d.

BREWSTER (SIR DAVID), WORKS BY. Post 8vo, cl. ex., 4s. 6d. each.
MORE WORLDS THAN ONE: Creed of Philosopher and Hope of Christian. Plates.
THE MARTYRS OF SCIENCE: GALILEO, TYCHO BRAHE and KEPLER. With Portraits.
LETTERS ON NATURAL MAGIC. With numerous Illustrations.

BRET HARTE, WORKS BY.

LIBRARY EDITION. Complete in Six Volumes, crown 8vo, cloth extra, **6s.** each.
BRET HARTE'S COLLECTED WORKS. Arranged and Revised by the Author.
Vol. I. COMPLETE POETICAL AND DRAMATIC WORKS. With Steel Portrait.
Vol. II. LUCK OF ROARING CAMP—BOHEMIAN PAPERS—AMERICAN LEGENDS.
Vol. III. TALES OF THE ARGONAUTS—EASTERN SKETCHES.
Vol. IV. GABRIEL CONROY.
Vol. V. STORIES—CONDENSED NOVELS, &c.
Vol. VI. TALES OF THE PACIFIC SLOPE.
Vol.VII. *is in preparation.* With a Portrait by JOHN PETTIE, R.A.

THE SELECT WORKS OF BRET HARTE, in Prose and Poetry. With Introductory
Essay by J. M. BELLEW, Portrait of Author, and 50 Illusts. Cr.8vo, cl. ex., **7s. 6d.**
BRET HARTE'S POETICAL WORKS. Hand-made paper & buckram. Cr.8vo, **4s.6d.**
THE QUEEN OF THE PIRATE ISLE. With 25 original Drawings by KATE
GREENAWAY, reproduced in Colours by EDMUND EVANS. Small 4to, cloth, **5s.**

Crown 8vo, cloth extra, **3s. 6d.** each.
A WAIF OF THE PLAINS. With 60 Illustrations by STANLEY L. WOOD.
A WARD OF THE GOLDEN GATE. With 59 Illustrations by STANLEY L. WOOD.
A SAPPHO OF GREEN SPRINGS, &c. With Two Illustrations by HUME NISBET.
COLONEL STARBOTTLE'S CLIENT, AND SOME OTHER PEOPLE. With a
Frontispiece by FRED. BARNARD.   [*Preparing.*

Post 8vo, illustrated boards, **2s.** each.

GABRIEL CONROY.	THE LUCK OF ROARING CAMP, &c.
AN HEIRESS OF RED DOG, &c.	CALIFORNIAN STORIES.

Post 8vo, illustrated boards, **2s.** each; cloth limp, **2s. 6d.** each.

FLIP.	MARUJA.	A PHYLLIS OF THE SIERRAS.

Fcap. 8vo picture cover, **1s.** each.

THE TWINS OF TABLE MOUNTAIN.	JEFF BRIGGS'S LOVE STORY.

BRILLAT-SAVARIN.—GASTRONOMY AS A FINE ART. By BRILLAT-
SAVARIN. Translated by R. E. ANDERSON, M.A. Post 8vo, half-bound, **2s.**

BRYDGES.—UNCLE SAM AT HOME. By HAROLD BRYDGES. Post
8vo, Illustrated boards, **2s.**; cloth limp, **2s. 6d.**

BUCHANAN'S (ROBERT) WORKS. Crown 8vo, cloth extra, **6s.** each.
SELECTED POEMS OF ROBERT BUCHANAN. With Frontispiece by T. DALZIEL.
THE EARTHQUAKE; or, Six Days and a Sabbath.
THE CITY OF DREAM: An Epic Poem. With Two Illustrations by P. MACNAB.
THE OUTCAST: A Rhyme for the Time. With 15 Illustrations by RUDOLF BLIND,
PETER MACNAB, and HUME NISBET. Small demy 8vo, cloth extra, **8s.**
ROBERT BUCHANAN'S COMPLETE POETICAL WORKS. With Steel-plate Por-
trait. Crown 8vo, cloth extra, **7s. 6d.**

Crown 8vo, cloth extra, **3s. 6d.** each; post 8vo, illustrated boards, **2s.** each.

THE SHADOW OF THE SWORD.	LOVE ME FOR EVER. Frontispiece.
A CHILD OF NATURE. Frontispiece.	ANNAN WATER.	FOXGLOVE MANOR.
GOD AND THE MAN. With 11 Illus-	THE NEW ABELARD.
trations by FRED. BARNARD.	MATT: A Story of a Caravan. Front.
THE MARTYRDOM OF MADELINE.	THE MASTER OF THE MINE. Front.
With Frontispiece by A. W. COOPER	THE HEIR OF LINNE.

BURTON (CAPTAIN).—THE BOOK OF THE SWORD: Being a
History of the Sword and its Use in all Countries, from the Earliest Times. By
RICHARD F. BURTON. With over 400 Illustrations. Square 8vo, cloth extra. **32s.**

BURTON (ROBERT).
THE ANATOMY OF MELANCHOLY: A New Edition, with translations of the
Classical Extracts. Demy 8vo, cloth extra, **7s. 6d.**
MELANCHOLY ANATOMISED Being an Abridgment, for popular use, of BURTON'S
ANATOMY OF MELANCHOLY. Post 8vo, cloth limp, **2s. 6d.**

CAINE (T. HALL), NOVELS BY. Crown 8vo, cloth extra, **3s. 6d.** each
post 8vo, illustrated boards, **2s.** each; cloth limp, **2s. 6d.** each.

SHADOW OF A CRIME.	A SON OF HAGAR.	THE DEEMSTER.

CAMERON (COMMANDER).—THE CRUISE OF THE "BLACK
PRINCE" PRIVATEER. By V. LOVETT CAMERON, R.N., C.B. With Two Illustrations by P. MACNAB. Crown 8vo, cloth extra, **5s.**; post 8vo, illustrated boards, **2s.**

CAMERON (MRS. H. LOVETT), NOVELS BY.
Crown 8vo, cloth extra, **3s. 6d.** each; post 8vo, illustrated boards, **2s.** each.

JULIET'S GUARDIAN.	DECEIVERS EVER.

CARLYLE (THOMAS) ON THE CHOICE OF BOOKS. With Life
by R. H. Shepherd, and Three Illustrations. Post 8vo, cloth extra, **1s. 6d.**
THE CORRESPONDENCE OF THOMAS CARLYLE AND RALPH WALDO
EMERSON, 1834 to 1872. Edited by Charles Eliot Norton. With Portraits.
Two Vols., crown 8vo, cloth extra, **24s.**

CARLYLE (JANE WELSH), LIFE OF. By Mrs. Alexander Ireland.
With Portrait and Facsimile Letter. Small demy 8vo, cloth extra, **7s. 6d.**

CHAPMAN'S (GEORGE) WORKS. Vol. I contains the Plays complete,
including the doubtful ones. Vol. II., the Poems and Minor Translations, with an
Introductory Essay by Algernon Charles Swinburne. Vol. III., the Translations
of the Iliad and Olyssey. Three Vols., crown 8vo, cloth extra, **6s.** each.

CHATTO AND JACKSON.—A TREATISE ON WOOD ENGRAVING,
Historical and Practical. By William Andrew Chatto and John Jackson. With
an Additional Chapter by Henry G. Bohn, and 450 fine Illusts. Large 4to hf.-bd., **28s.**

CHAUCER FOR CHILDREN: A Golden Key. By Mrs. H. R. Haweis.
With 8 Coloured Plates and 30 Woodcuts. Small 4to, cloth extra, **6s.**
CHAUCER FOR SCHOOLS. By Mrs. H. R. Haweis. Demy 8vo, cloth limo, **2s. 6d.**

CLARE.—FOR THE LOVE OF A LASS: A Tale of Tynedale. By
Austin Clare. Post 8vo, picture boards, **2s.**; cloth limp, **2s. 6d.**

CLIVE (MRS. ARCHER), NOVELS BY. Post 8vo, illust. boards, **2s.** each.
PAUL FERROLL. | WHY PAUL FERROLL KILLED HIS WIFE.

CLODD.—MYTHS AND DREAMS. By Edward Clodd, F.R.A.S.
Second Edition, Revised. Crown 8vo, cloth extra, **3s. 6d.**

COBBAN.—THE CURE OF SOULS: A Story. By J. Maclaren
Cobban. Post 8vo, illustrated boards, **2s.**

COLEMAN (JOHN), WORKS BY.
PLAYERS AND PLAYWRIGHTS I HAVE KNOWN. Two Vols., 8vo, cloth, **24s.**
CURLY: An Actor's Story. With 21 Illusts. by J. C. Dollman. Cr. 8vo, cl., **1s. 6d.**

COLLINS (C. ALLSTON).—THE BAR SINISTER. Post 8vo, **2s.**

COLLINS (MORTIMER AND FRANCES), NOVELS BY.
Crown 8vo, cloth extra, **3s. 6d.** each; post 8vo, illustrated boards, **2s.** each.
SWEET ANNE PAGE. | FROM MIDNIGHT TO MIDNIGHT. | TRANSMIGRATION.
BLACKSMITH AND SCHOLAR. | YOU PLAY ME FALSE. | VILLAGE COMEDY.
Post 8vo, illustrated boards, **2s.** each.
A FIGHT WITH FORTUNE. | SWEET AND TWENTY. | FRANCES.

COLLINS (WILKIE), NOVELS BY.
Cr. 8vo, cl. ex., **3s. 6d.** each; post 8vo, illust. bds., **2s.** each; cl. limp, **2s. 6d.** each.
ANTONINA. With a Frontispiece by Sir John Gilbert, R.A.
BASIL. Illustrated by Sir John Gilbert, R.A., and J. Mahoney.
HIDE AND SEEK. Illustrated by Sir John Gilbert, R.A., and J. Mahoney.
AFTER DARK. With Illustrations by A. B. Houghton.
THE DEAD SECRET. With a Frontispiece by Sir John Gilbert, R.A.
QUEEN OF HEARTS. With a Frontispiece by Sir John Gilbert, R.A.
THE WOMAN IN WHITE. With Illusts. by Sir J. Gilbert, R.A., and F. A. Fraser.
NO NAME. With Illustrations by Sir J. E. Millais, R.A., and A. W. Cooper.
MY MISCELLANIES. With a Steel-plate Portrait of Wilkie Collins.
ARMADALE. With Illustrations by G. H. Thomas.
THE MOONSTONE. With Illustrations by G. Du Maurier and F. A. Fraser.
MAN AND WIFE. With Illustrations by William Small.
POOR MISS FINCH. Illustrated by G. Du Maurier and Edward Hughes.
MISS OR MRS.? With Illusts. by S. L. Fildes, R.A., and Henry Woods, A.R.A.
THE NEW MAGDALEN. Illustrated by G. Du Maurier and C. S. Reinhardt.
THE FROZEN DEEP. Illustrated by G. Du Maurier and J. Mahoney.
THE LAW AND THE LADY. Illusts. by S. L. Fildes, R.A., and Sydney Hall.
THE TWO DESTINIES.
THE HAUNTED HOTEL. Illustrated by Arthur Hopkins.
THE FALLEN LEAVES. | HEART AND SCIENCE. | THE EVIL GENIUS.
JEZEBEL'S DAUGHTER. | "I SAY NO." | LITTLE NOVELS.
THE BLACK ROBE. | A ROGUE'S LIFE. | THE LEGACY OF CAIN.
BLIND LOVE. With Preface by Walter Besant, and Illusts. by A. Forestier.

COLLINS (JOHN CHURTON, M.A.), BOOKS BY.
ILLUSTRATIONS OF TENNYSON. Crown 8vo, cloth extra, **6s.** [*Shortly*
A MONOGRAPH ON DEAN SWIFT. Crown 8vo, cloth extra, **8s.** [*Shortly*

COLMAN'S HUMOROUS WORKS: "Broad Grins," "My Nightgow
and Slippers," and other Humorous Works of GEORGE COLMAN. With Life I
G. B. BUCKSTONE, and Frontispiece by HOGARTH. Crown 8vo, cloth extra. **7s. 6**

COLQUHOUN.—EVERY INCH A SOLDIER: A Novel. By M
COLQUHOUN. Post 8vo, illustrated boards, **2s.**

CONVALESCENT COOKERY: A Family Handbook. By CATHERIN
RYAN. Crown 8vo, **1s.**; cloth limp, **1s. 6d.**

CONWAY (MONCURE D.), WORKS BY.
DEMONOLOGY AND DEVIL-LORE. With 65 Illustrations, Third Edition. Tw
Vols., demy 8vo, cloth extra, **28s.**
A NECKLACE OF STORIES. 25 Illusts. by W. J. HENNESSY. Sq. 8vo, cloth, **6s.**
PINE AND PALM: A Novel. Two Vols., crown 8vo, cloth extra. **21s.**
GEORGE WASHINGTON'S RULES OF CIVILITY Traced to their Sources an
Restored. Fcap. 8vo, Japanese vellum, **2s. 6d.**

COOK (DUTTON), NOVELS BY.
PAUL FOSTER'S DAUGHTER. Cr. 8vo, cl. ex., **3s. 6d.**; post 8vo, illust. boards, 2s
LEO. Post 8vo, illustrated boards, **2s.**

CORNWALL.—POPULAR ROMANCES OF THE WEST OF ENG
LAND; or, The Drolls, Traditions, and Superstitions of Old Cornwall. Collecte
by ROBERT HUNT, F.R.S. Two Steel-plates by GEO. CRUIKSHANK. Cr. 8vo cl., **7s. 6d**

COTES.—TWO GIRLS ON A BARGE. By V. CECIL COTES. Wit
44 Illustrations by F. H. TOWNSEND. Crown 8vo, cloth extra, **3s. 6d.**

CRADDOCK.—THE PROPHET OF THE GREAT SMOKY MOUN
TAINS. By CHARLES EGBERT CRADDOCK. Post 8vo, illust bds., **2s.**; cl. limp, **2s. 6d**

CRUIKSHANK'S COMIC ALMANACK, Complete in Two SERIES
The FIRST from 1835 to 1843; the SECOND from 1844 to 1853. A Gathering c
the BEST HUMOUR of THACKERAY, HOOD, MAYHEW, ALBERT SMITH, A'BECKETT
ROBERT BROUGH, &c. With numerous Steel Engravings and Woodcuts by CRUI
SHANK, HINE, LANDELLS, &c. Two Vols., crown 8vo, cloth gilt, **7s. 6d.** each.
THE LIFE OF GEORGE CRUIKSHANK. By BLANCHARD JERROLD. With 5
Illustrations and a Bibliography Crown 8vo, cloth extra, **7s. 6d.**

CUMMING (C. F. GORDON), WORKS BY. Demy 8vo, cl. ex., **8s. 6d.** each
IN THE HEBRIDES. With Autotype Facsimile and 23 Illustrations.
IN THE HIMALAYAS AND ON THE INDIAN PLAINS. With 42 Illustrations.
VIA CORNWALL TO EGYPT. With Photogravure Frontis. Demy 8vo, cl., **7s. 6d**

CUSSANS.—A HANDBOOK OF HERALDRY; with Instructions fo
Tracing Pedigrees and Deciphering Ancient MSS., &c. By JOHN E. CUSSANS. Wit
408 Woodcuts, Two Coloured and Two Plain Plates. Crown 8vo, cloth extra, **7s. 6d**

CYPLES(W.)—HEARTS of GOLD. Cr. 8vo, cl. **3s. 6d.**; post 8vo, bds., 2s

DANIEL.—MERRIE ENGLAND IN THE OLDEN TIME. By GEORG
DANIEL. With Illustrations by ROBERT CRUIKSHANK. Crown 8vo, cloth extra, **3s. 6d**

DAUDET.—THE EVANGELIST; or, Port Salvation. By ALPHONS
DAUDET. Crown 8vo, cloth extra **3s. 6d.**; post 8vo, illustrated boards, **2s.**

DAVENANT.—HINTS FOR PARENTS ON THE CHOICE OF A PRO
FESSION FOR THEIR SONS. By F. DAVENANT, M.A. Post 8vo, **1s.**; cl., **1s. 6d**

DAVIES (DR. N. E. YORKE-), WORKS BY.
Crown 8vo, **1s.** each; cloth limp, **1s. 6d.** each
ONE THOUSAND MEDICAL MAXIMS AND SURGICAL HINTS.
NURSERY HINTS: A Mother's Guide in Health and Disease.
FOODS FOR THE FAT: A Treatise on Corpulency, and a Dietary for its Cure.
AIDS TO LONG LIFE. Crown 8vo, **2s.**; cloth limp, **2s. 6d.**

DAVIES' (SIR JOHN) COMPLETE POETICAL WORKS, including
Psalms I. to L. in Verse, and other hitherto Unpublished MSS., for the first time
Collected and Edited, with Memorial-Introduction and Notes, by the Rev. A. B
GROSART, D.D. Two Vols., crown 8vo. cloth boards, **12s.**

DAWSON.—THE FOUNTAIN OF YOUTH: A Novel of Adventure.
By ERASMUS DAWSON, M.B. Edited by PAUL DEVON. With Two Illustrations by
HUME NISBET. Crown 8vo, cloth extra, **3s. 6d.**

DE GUERIN.—THE JOURNAL OF MAURICE DE GUERIN. Edited by G. S. TREBUTIEN. With a Memoir by SAINTE-BEUVE. Translated from the 20th French Edition by JESSIE P. FROTHINGHAM. Fcap. 8vo, half-bound, 2s. 6d.

DE MAISTRE.—A JOURNEY ROUND MY ROOM. By XAVIER DE MAISTRE. Translated by HENRY ATTWELL. Post 8vo, cloth limp, 2s. 6d.

DE MILLE.—A CASTLE IN SPAIN. By JAMES DE MILLE. With a Frontispiece. Crown 8vo, cloth extra, 3s. 6d.; post 8vo, illustrated boards, 2s.

DERBY (THE).—THE BLUE RIBBON OF THE TURF: A Chronicle of the RACE FOR THE DERBY, from Diomed to Donovan. With Notes on the Winning Horses, the Men who trained them, Jockeys who rode them, and Gentlemen to whom they belonged; also Notices of the Betting and Betting Men of the period, and Brief Accounts of THE OAKS. By LOUIS HENRY CURZON. Cr. 8vo, cloth extra, 6s.

DERWENT (LEITH), NOVELS BY. Cr. 8vo, cl., 3s. 6d. ea.; post 8vo, bds., 2s. ea.

OUR LADY OF TEARS. | CIRCE'S LOVERS.

DICKENS (CHARLES), NOVELS BY. Post 8vo, illustrated boards, 2s. each.

SKETCHES BY BOZ. | NICHOLAS NICKLEBY.
THE PICKWICK PAPERS. | OLIVER TWIST.

THE SPEECHES OF CHARLES DICKENS, 1841–1870. With a New Bibliography. Edited by RICHARD SHEPHERD. Crown 8vo, cloth extra, 6s.—Also a SMALLER EDITION, in the Mayfair Library, post 8vo, cloth limp, 2s. 6d.

ABOUT ENGLAND WITH DICKENS. By ALFRED RIMMER. With 57 Illustrations by C. A. VANDERHOOF, ALFRED RIMMER, and others. Sq. 8vo, cloth extra, 7s. 6d.

DICTIONARIES.

A DICTIONARY OF MIRACLES: Imitative, Realistic, and Dogmatic. By the Rev. E. C. BREWER, LL.D. Crown 8vo, cloth extra, 7s. 6d.

THE READER'S HANDBOOK OF ALLUSIONS, REFERENCES, PLOTS, AND STORIES. By the Rev. E. C. BREWER, LL.D. With an ENGLISH BIBLIOGRAPHY. Fifteenth Thousand. Crown 8vo, cloth extra, 7s. 6d.

AUTHORS AND THEIR WORKS, WITH THE DATES. Cr. 8vo, cloth limp, 2s.

FAMILIAR SHORT SAYINGS OF GREAT MEN. With Historical and Explanatory Notes. By SAMUEL A. BENT, A. M. Crown 8vo, cloth extra, 7s. 6d.

SLANG DICTIONARY: Etymological, Historical, and Anecdotal. Cr. 8vo, cl., 6s. 6d.

WOMEN OF THE DAY: A Biographical Dictionary. By F. HAYS. Cr. 8vo, cl., 5s.

WORDS, FACTS, AND PHRASES: A Dictionary of Curious, Quaint, and Out-of-the-Way Matters. By ELIEZER EDWARDS. Crown 8vo, cloth extra, 7s. 6d.

DIDEROT.—THE PARADOX OF ACTING. Translated, with Annotations, from Diderot's "Le Paradoxe sur le Comédien," by WALTER HERRIES POLLOCK. With a Preface by HENRY IRVING. Crown 8vo, parchment, 4s. 6d.

DOBSON (AUSTIN), WORKS BY.

THOMAS BEWICK & HIS PUPILS. With 95 Illustrations. Square 8vo, cloth, 6s.

FOUR FRENCHWOMEN. MADEMOISELLE DE CORDAY; MADAME ROLAND; THE PRINCESS DE LAMBALLE; MADAME DE GENLIS. Fcap. 8vo, hf.-roxburghe, 2s. 6d.

DOBSON (W. T.), WORKS BY. Post 8vo, cloth limp, 2s. 6d. each.

LITERARY FRIVOLITIES, FANCIES, FOLLIES, AND FROLICS.
POETICAL INGENUITIES AND ECCENTRICITIES.

DONOVAN (DICK), DETECTIVE STORIES BY.

Post 8vo, illustrated boards, 2s. each; cloth limp, 2s. 6d. each.

THE MAN-HUNTER. | TRACKED AND TAKEN.
CAUGHT AT LAST! | WHO POISONED HETTY DUNCAN?
A DETECTIVE'S TRIUMPHS.

THE MAN FROM MANCHESTER. With 23 Illustrations. Crown 8vo, cloth, 6s.; post 8vo, illustrated boards, 2s.

DOYLE (A. CONAN, Author of "Micah Clarke"), **NOVELS BY.**

THE FIRM OF GIRDLESTONE. Crown 8vo, cloth extra, 6s.

STRANGE SECRETS. Told by CONAN DOYLE, PERCY FITZGERALD, FLORENCE MARRYAT, &c. Cr. 8vo, cl. ex., Eight Illusts., 6s.; post 8vo, illust. bds., 2s.

DRAMATISTS, THE OLD. With Vignette Portraits. Cr. 8vo, cl. ex., 6s. per Vol.

BEN JONSON'S WORKS. With Notes Critical and Explanatory, and a Biographical Memoir by WM. GIFFORD. Edited by Col. CUNNINGHAM. Three Vols.

CHAPMAN'S WORKS. Complete in Three Vols. Vol. I. contains the Plays complete; Vol. II., Poems and Minor Translations, with an Introductory Essay by A. C. SWINBURNE; Vol. III., Translations of the Iliad and Odyssey.

MARLOWE'S WORKS. Edited, with Notes, by Col. CUNNINGHAM. One Vol.

MASSINGER'S PLAYS. From GIFFORD'S Text. Edit. by Col. CUNNINGHAM. One Vol.

DUNCAN (SARA JEANNETTE), WORKS BY.
Crown 8vo, cloth extra, **7s. 6d.** each.
A SOCIAL DEPARTURE: How Orthodocia and I Went round the World by Ourselves. With 111 Illustrations by F. H. TOWNSEND.
AN AMERICAN GIRL IN LONDON. With 80 Illustrations by F. H. TOWNSEND.

DYER.—THE FOLK-LORE OF PLANTS. By Rev. T. F. THISELTON DYER, M.A. Crown 8vo, cloth extra, **6s.**

EARLY ENGLISH POETS. Edited, with Introductions and Annotations, by Rev. A. B. GROSART, D.D. Crown 8vo, cloth boards, **6s.** per Volume.
FLETCHER'S (GILES) COMPLETE POEMS. One Vol.
DAVIES' (SIR JOHN) COMPLETE POETICAL WORKS. Two Vols.
HERRICK'S (ROBERT) COMPLETE COLLECTED POEMS. Three Vols.
SIDNEY'S (SIR PHILIP) COMPLETE POETICAL WORKS. Three Vols.

EDGCUMBE.—ZEPHYRUS : A Holiday in Brazil and on the River Plate. By E. R. PEARCE EDGCUMBE. With 41 Illustrations. Crown 8vo, cloth extra, **5s.**

EDWARDES (MRS. ANNIE), NOVELS BY:
A POINT OF HONOUR. Post 8vo, illustrated boards, **2s.**
ARCHIE LOVELL. Crown 8vo, cloth extra, **3s. 6d.** ; post 8vo, illust. boards, **2s.**

EDWARDS (ELIEZER).—WORDS, FACTS, AND PHRASES: A Dictionary of Curious, Quaint, and Out-of-the-Way Matters. By ELIEZER EDWARDS. Crown 8vo, cloth extra, **7s. 6d.**

EDWARDS (M. BETHAM-), NOVELS BY.
KITTY. Post 8vo, illustrated boards, **2s.** ; cloth limp, **2s. 6d.**
FELICIA. Post 8vo, illustrated boards, **2s.**

EGGLESTON (EDWARD).—ROXY : A Novel. Post 8vo, illust. bds., 2s.

EMANUEL.—ON DIAMONDS AND PRECIOUS STONES: Their History, Value, and Properties ; with Simple Tests for ascertaining their Reality. By HARRY EMANUEL, F.R.G.S. With Illustrations, tinted and plain. Cr. 8vo, cl. ex., **6s.**

ENGLISHMAN'S HOUSE, THE: A Practical Guide to all interested in Selecting or Building a House; with Estimates of Cost, Quantities, &c. By C. J. RICHARDSON. With Coloured Frontispiece and 600 Illusts. Crown 8vo, cloth, **7s. 6d.**

EWALD (ALEX. CHARLES, F.S.A.), WORKS BY.
THE LIFE AND TIMES OF PRINCE CHARLES STUART, Count of Albany (THE YOUNG PRETENDER). With a Portrait. Crown 8vo, cloth extra, **7s. 6d.**
STORIES FROM THE STATE PAPERS. With an Autotype. Crown 8vo, cloth, **6s.**

EYES, OUR : How to Preserve Them from Infancy to Old Age. By JOHN BROWNING, F.R.A.S. With 70 Illusts. Eighteenth Thousand. Crown 8vo, **1s.**

FAMILIAR SHORT SAYINGS OF GREAT MEN. By SAMUEL ARTHUR BENT, A.M. Fifth Edition, Revised and Enlarged. Crown 8vo, cloth extra, **7s. 6d.**

FARADAY (MICHAEL), WORKS BY. Post 8vo, cloth extra, **4s. 6d.** each.
THE CHEMICAL HISTORY OF A CANDLE: Lectures delivered before a Juvenile Audience. Edited by WILLIAM CROOKES, F.C.S. With numerous Illustrations.
ON THE VARIOUS FORCES OF NATURE, AND THEIR RELATIONS TO EACH OTHER. Edited by WILLIAM CROOKES, F.C.S. With Illustrations.

FARRER (J. ANSON), WORKS BY.
MILITARY MANNERS AND CUSTOMS. Crown 8vo, cloth extra, **6s.**
WAR: Three Essays, reprinted from "Military Manners." Cr. 8vo, **1s.** ; cl. **1s. 6d.**

FENN (MANVILLE).—THE NEW MISTRESS : A Novel. By G. MANVILLE FENN, Author of "Double Cunning," &c. Crown 8vo, cloth extra, **3s. 6d.**

FICTION.—A CATALOGUE OF NEARLY SIX HUNDRED WORKS OF FICTION published by CHATTO & WINDUS, with a Short Critical Notice of each (40 pages, demy 8vo), will be sent free upon application.

FIN-BEC.—THE CUPBOARD PAPERS : Observations on the Art of Living and Dining. By FIN-BEC. Post 8vo, cloth limp, **2s. 6d.**

FIREWORKS, THE COMPLETE ART OF MAKING ; or, The Pyrotechnist's Treasury. By THOMAS KENTISH. With 267 Illustrations. Cr. 8vo, cl., **5s.**

FITZGERALD (PERCY, M.A., F.S.A.), WORKS BY.
THE WORLD BEHIND THE SCENES. Crown 8vo, cloth extra, 3s. 6d.
LITTLE ESSAYS: Passages from Letters of CHARLES LAMB. Post 8vo, cl., 2s. 6d.
A DAY'S TOUR: Journey through France and Belgium. With Sketches. Cr. 4to, 1s.
FATAL ZERO. Crown 8vo, cloth extra. 3s. 6d.; post 8vo, illustrated boards, 2s.

Post 8vo, illustrated boards, 2s. each.
BELLA DONNA. | **LADY OF BRANTOME.** | **THE SECOND MRS. TILLOTSON.**
POLLY. | **NEVER FORGOTTEN.** | **SEVENTY-FIVE BROOKE STREET.**
LIFE OF JAMES BOSWELL (of Auchinleck). With an Account of his Savings,
Doings, and Writings; and Four Portraits. Two Vols., demy 8vo, cloth, 24s.

FLAMMARION.—URANIA : A Romance. By CAMILLE FLAMMARION.
Translated by AUGUSTA RICE STETSON. With 90 Illustrations by DE BIELER,
MYRBACH, and GAMBARD. Crown 8vo, cloth extra, 5s.

FLETCHER'S (GILES, B.D.) COMPLETE POEMS : Christ's Victorie
in Heaven, Christ's Victorie on Earth, Christ's Triumph over Death, and Minor
Poems. With Notes by Rev. A. B. GROSART, D.D. Crown 8vo, cloth boards, 6s.

FLUDYER (HARRY) AT CAMBRIDGE: A Series of Family Letters.
Post 8vo, picture cover. 1s.; cloth limp, 1s. 6d.

FONBLANQUE (ALBANY).—FILTHY LUCRE. Post 8vo, illust. bds., 2s.

FRANCILLON (R. E.), NOVELS BY.
Crown 8vo, cloth extra. 3s. 6d. each; post 8vo, illustrated boards, 2s. each.
ONE BY ONE. | QUEEN COPHETUA. | A REAL QUEEN. | KING OR KNAVE?
OLYMPIA. Post 8vo, illust. bds., 2s. | ESTHER'S GLOVE. Fcap. 8vo, pict. cover, 1s.
ROMANCES OF THE LAW. Crown 8vo, cloth, 6s.; post 8vo, illust. boards, 2s.

FREDERIC (HAROLD), NOVELS BY.
SETH'S BROTHER'S WIFE. Post 8vo, illustrated boards, 2s.
THE LAWTON GIRL. With Frontispiece by F. BARNARD. Cr. 8vo, cloth ex., 6s.;
post 8vo, illustrated boards, 2s.

FRENCH LITERATURE, A HISTORY OF. By HENRY VAN LAUN.
Three Vols., demy 8vo, cloth boards, 7s. 6d. each.

FRENZENY.—FIFTY YEARS ON THE TRAIL: Adventures of JOHN
Y. NELSON, Scout, Guide, and Interpreter. By HARRINGTON O'REILLY. With 100
Illustrations by PAUL FRENZENY. Crown 8vo, cloth extra, 3s. 6d.

FRERE.—PANDURANG HARI; or, Memoirs of a Hindoo. With Pre-
face by Sir BARTLE FRERE. Crown 8vo, cloth, 3s. 6d.; post 8vo, illust. bds., 2s.

FRISWELL (HAIN).—ONE OF TWO: A Novel. Post 8vo, illust. bds., 2s.

FROST (THOMAS), WORKS BY. Crown 8vo, cloth extra, 3s. 6d. each.
CIRCUS LIFE AND CIRCUS CELEBRITIES. | LIVES OF THE CONJURERS.
THE OLD SHOWMEN AND THE OLD LONDON FAIRS.

FRY'S (HERBERT) ROYAL GUIDE TO THE LONDON CHARITIES.
Showing their Name, Date of Foundation, Objects, Income, Officials, &c. Edited
by JOHN LANE. Published Annually. Crown 8vo, cloth, 1s. 6d.

GARDENING BOOKS. Post 8vo, 1s. each; cloth limp, 1s. 6d. each.
A YEAR'S WORK IN GARDEN AND GREENHOUSE: Practical Advice as to the
Management of the Flower, Fruit, and Frame Garden. By GEORGE GLENNY.
OUR KITCHEN GARDEN: Plants, and How we Cook Them. By TOM JERROLD.
HOUSEHOLD HORTICULTURE. By TOM and JANE JERROLD. Illustrated.
THE GARDEN THAT PAID THE RENT. By TOM JERROLD.

MY GARDEN WILD, AND WHAT I GREW THERE. By FRANCIS G. HEATH.
Crown 8vo, cloth extra, gilt edges, 6s.

GARRETT.—THE CAPEL GIRLS: A Novel. By EDWARD GARRETT.
Crown 8vo, cloth extra 3s. 6d.; post 8vo, illustrated boards, 2s.

GENTLEMAN'S MAGAZINE, THE. 1s. Monthly. In addition to the
Articles upon subjects in Literature, Science, and Art, for which this Magazine has
so high a reputation, "TABLE TALK" by SYLVANUS URBAN appears monthly.
. Bound Volumes for recent years kept in stock, 8s. 6d. each. Cases for binding, 2s.

GENTLEMAN'S ANNUAL, THE. Published Annually in November. 1s.
The 1891 Annual is written by T. W. SPEIGHT, Author of "The Mysteries of Heron
Dyke," and is entitled BACK TO LIFE.

GERMAN POPULAR STORIES. Collected by the Brothers GRIMM and Translated by EDGAR TAYLOR. With Introduction by JOHN RUSKIN, and 22 Steel Plates by GEORGE CRUIKSHANK. Square 8vo, cloth, 6s. 6d.; gilt edges, 7s. 6d.

GIBBON (CHARLES), NOVELS BY. Crown 8vo, cloth extra, 3s. 6d. each; post 8vo, illustrated boards, 2s. each.

ROBIN GRAY.	LOVING A DREAM.	OF HIGH DEGREE.
THE FLOWER OF THE FOREST.	IN HONOUR BOUND.
THE GOLDEN SHAFT.	

Post 8vo, illustrated boards, 2s. each.

THE DEAD HEART.	IN LOVE AND WAR.
FOR LACK OF GOLD.	A HEART'S PROBLEM.
WHAT WILL THE WORLD SAY?	BY MEAD AND STREAM.
FOR THE KING.	THE BRAES OF YARROW.
QUEEN OF THE MEADOW.	FANCY FREE.	A HARD KNOT.
IN PASTURES GREEN.	HEART'S DELIGHT.	BLOOD-MONEY.

GIBNEY (SOMERVILLE).—SENTENCED! Cr. 8vo, 1s. ; cl., 1s. 6d.

GILBERT (WILLIAM), NOVELS BY. Post 8vo, illustrated boards. 2s. each.

DR. AUSTIN'S GUESTS.	JAMES DUKE, COSTERMONGER.
THE WIZARD OF THE MOUNTAIN.	

GILBERT (W. S.), ORIGINAL PLAYS BY. In Two Series, each complete in itself, price 2s. 6d. each.

The FIRST SERIES contains: The Wicked World—Pygmalion and Galatea—Charity—The Princess—The Palace of Truth—Trial by Jury. The SECOND SERIES: Broken Hearts—Engaged—Sweethearts—Gretchen—Dan'l Druce—Tom Cobb—H.M.S. "Pinafore"—The Sorcerer—Pirates of Penzance.

EIGHT ORIGINAL COMIC OPERAS written by W. S. GILBERT. Containing: The Sorcerer—H.M.S. "Pinafore"—Pirates of Penzance—Iolanthe—Patience—Princess Ida—The Mikado—Trial by Jury. Demy 8vo, cloth limp, 2s. 6d.

THE "GILBERT AND SULLIVAN" BIRTHDAY BOOK: Quotations for Every Day in the Year, Selected from Plays by W. S. GILBERT set to Music by Sir A. SULLIVAN. Compiled by ALEX. WATSON. Royal 16mo. Jap. leather, 2s. 6d.

GLANVILLE (ERNEST), NOVELS BY.
THE LOST HEIRESS: A Tale of Love, Battle and Adventure. With 2 Illusts. by HUME NISBET. Cr. 8vo, cloth extra, 3s. 6d.
THE FOSSICKER. With Frontispiece and Vignette by HUME NISBET. Crown 8vo, cloth extra, 3s. 6d.

GLENNY.—A YEAR'S WORK IN GARDEN AND GREENHOUSE: Practical Advice to Amateur Gardeners as to the Management of the Flower, Fruit, and Frame Garden. By GEORGE GLENNY. Post 8vo, 1s.; cloth limp, 1s. 6d.

GODWIN.—LIVES OF THE NECROMANCERS. By WILLIAM GODWIN. Post 8vo, cloth limp, 2s.

GOLDEN TREASURY OF THOUGHT, THE: An Encyclopædia of QUOTATIONS. Edited by THEODORE TAYLOR. Crown 8vo, cloth gilt, 7s. 6d.

GOWING.—FIVE THOUSAND MILES IN A SLEDGE: A Midwinter Journey Across Siberia. By LIONEL F. GOWING. With 30 Illustrations by C. J. UREN, and a Map by E. WELLER. Large crown 8vo, cloth extra, 8s.

GRAHAM.—THE PROFESSOR'S WIFE: A Story. By LEONARD GRAHAM. Fcap. 8vo, picture cover, 1s.

GREEKS AND ROMANS, THE LIFE OF THE, described from Antique Monuments. By ERNST GUHL and W. KONER. Edited by Dr. F. HUEFFER. With 545 Illustrations. Large crown 8vo, cloth extra, 7s. 6d.

GREENWOOD (JAMES), WORKS BY. Cr. 8vo, cloth extra, 3s. 6d. each.

THE WILDS OF LONDON.	LOW-LIFE DEEPS.

GREVILLE (HENRY), NOVELS BY:
NIKANOR. Translated by ELIZA E. CHASE. With 8 Illusts. Cr. 8vo, cl. extra, 6s.
A NOBLE WOMAN. Translated by ALBERT D. VANDAM. Crown 8vo, cloth extra, 5s.; post 8vo, illustrated boards, 2s.

HABBERTON (JOHN, Author of "Helen's Babies"), **NOVELS BY.** Post 8vo, illustrated boards 2s. each; cloth limp, 2s. 6d. each.

BRUETON'S BAYOU.	COUNTRY LUCK.

HAIR, THE: Its Treatment in Health, Weakness, and Disease. Translated from the German of Dr. J. Pincus. Crown 8vo, **1s.**; cloth limp, **1s. 6d.**

HAKE (DR. THOMAS GORDON), POEMS BY. Cr. 8vo, cl. ex., **6s.** each.
NEW SYMBOLS. | LEGENDS OF THE MORROW. | THE SERPENT PLAY.
MAIDEN ECSTASY. Small 4to, cloth extra, **8s.**

HALL.—SKETCHES OF IRISH CHARACTER. By Mrs. S. C. Hall. With numerous Illustrations on Steel and Wood by Maclise, Gilbert, Harvey, and George Cruikshank. Medium 8vo, cloth extra, **7s. 6d.**

HALLIDAY (ANDR.).—EVERY-DAY PAPERS. Post 8vo, bds., **2s.**

HANDWRITING, THE PHILOSOPHY OF. With over 100 Facsimiles and Explanatory Text. By Don Felix de Salamanca. Post 8vo, cloth limp, **2s. 6d.**

HANKY-PANKY: A Collection of Very Easy Tricks, Very Difficult Tricks, White Magic, Sleight of Hand, &c. Edited by W. H. Cremer. With 200 Illustrations. Crown 8vo, cloth extra, **4s. 6d.**

HARDY (LADY DUFFUS).—PAUL WYNTER' SACRIFICE. By Lady Duffus Hardy. Post 8vo, illustrated boards, **2s.**

HARDY (THOMAS).—UNDER THE GREENWOOD TREE. By Thomas Hardy, Author of "Far from the Madding Crowd." Post 8vo, illust. bds., **2s.**

HARWOOD.—THE TENTH EARL. By J. Berwick Harwood. Post 8vo, illustrated boards, **2s.**

HAWEIS (MRS. H. R.), WORKS BY. Square 8vo, cloth extra, **6s.** each.
THE ART OF BEAUTY. With Coloured Frontispiece and 91 Illustrations.
THE ART OF DECORATION. With Coloured Frontispiece and 74 Illustrations.
CHAUCER FOR CHILDREN. With 8 Coloured Plates and 30 Woodcuts.
THE ART OF DRESS. With 32 Illustrations. Post 8vo, **1s.**; cloth, **1s. 6d.**
CHAUCER FOR SCHOOLS. Demy 8vo, cloth limp, **2s. 6d.**

HAWEIS (Rev. H. R., M.A.).—AMERICAN HUMORISTS: Washington Irving, Oliver Wendell Holmes, James Russell Lowell, Artemus Ward, Mark Twain, and Bret Harte. Third Edition. Crown 8vo, cloth extra, **6s.**

HAWLEY SMART.—WITHOUT LOVE OR LICENCE: A Novel. By Hawley Smart. Crown 8vo, cloth extra, **3s. 6d.**

HAWTHORNE.—OUR OLD HOME. By Nathaniel Hawthorne. Annotated with Passages from the Author's Note-book, and Illustrated with 31 Photogravures. Two Vols., crown 8vo, buckram, gilt top, **15s.**

HAWTHORNE (JULIAN), NOVELS BY.
Crown 8vo, cloth extra, **3s. 6d.** each; post 8vo, illustrated boards, **2s.** each.
GARTH. | ELLICE QUENTIN. | BEATRIX RANDOLPH. | DUST.
SEBASTIAN STROME. | DAVID POINDEXTER.
FORTUNE'S FOOL. | THE SPECTRE OF THE CAMERA.
Post 8vo, illustrated boards, **2s.** each.
MISS CADOGNA. | LOVE—OR A NAME.
MRS. GAINSBOROUGH'S DIAMONDS. Fcap. 8vo, illustrated cover, **1s.**
A DREAM AND A FORGETTING. Post 8vo, cloth limp, **1s. 6d.**

HAYS.—WOMEN OF THE DAY: A Biographical Dictionary of Notable Contemporaries. By Frances Hays. Crown 8vo, cloth extra, **5s.**

HEATH.—MY GARDEN WILD, AND WHAT I GREW THERE. By Francis George Heath. Crown 8vo, cloth extra, gilt edges, **6s.**

HELPS (SIR ARTHUR), WORKS BY. Post 8vo, cloth limp, **2s. 6d.** each.
ANIMALS AND THEIR MASTERS. | SOCIAL PRESSURE.
IVAN DE BIRON: A Novel. Cr. 8vo, cl. extra, **3s. 6d.**; post 8vo, illust. bds., **2s.**

HENDERSON.—AGATHA PAGE: A Novel. By Isaac Henderson. Crown 8vo, cloth extra, **3s. 6d.**

HERMAN.—A LEADING LADY. By Henry Herman, joint-Author of "The Bishops' Bible." Post 8vo, cloth extra, **2s. 6d.**

HERRICK'S (ROBERT) HESPERIDES, NOBLE NUMBERS, AND COMPLETE COLLECTED POEMS. With Memorial-Introduction and Notes by the Rev. A. B. Grosart, D.D.; Steel Portrait, &c   Three Vols., crown 8vo, cl. bds., 18s.

HERTZKA.—FREELAND: A Social Anticipation.   By Dr. Theodor Hertzka. Translated by Arthur Ransom. Crown 8vo, cloth extra, 6s.

HESSE-WARTEGG.—TUNIS: The Land and the People. By Chevalier Ernst von Hesse-Wartegg. With 22 Illustrations. Cr. 8vo, cloth extra, 3s. 6d.

HINDLEY (CHARLES), WORKS BY.
TAVERN ANECDOTES AND SAYINGS: Including the Origin of Signs, and Reminiscences connected with Taverns, Coffee Houses, Clubs, &c. With Illustrations. Crown 8vo, cloth extra, 3s. 6d.
THE LIFE AND ADVENTURES OF A CHEAP JACK. By One of the Fraternity. Edited by Charles Hindley. Crown 8vo, cloth extra, 3s. 6d.

HOEY.—THE LOVER'S CREED. By Mrs. Cashel Hoey. Post 8vo, illustrated boards, 2s.

HOLLINGSHEAD (JOHN).—NIAGARA SPRAY. Crown 8vo, 1s.

HOLMES.—THE SCIENCE OF VOICE PRODUCTION AND VOICE PRESERVATION: A Popular Manual for the Use of Speakers and Singers. By Gordon Holmes, M.D. With Illustrations. Crown 8vo, 1s.; cloth, 1s. 6d.

HOLMES (OLIVER WENDELL), WORKS BY.
THE AUTOCRAT OF THE BREAKFAST-TABLE. Illustrated by J. Gordon Thomson. Post 8vo, cloth limp, 2s. 6d.—Another Edition, in smaller type, with an Introduction by G. A. Sala. Post 8vo, cloth limp, 2s.
THE PROFESSOR AT THE BREAKFAST-TABLE. Post 8vo, cloth limp, 2s.

HOOD'S (THOMAS) CHOICE WORKS, in Prose and Verse. With Life of the Author, Portrait, and 200 Illustrations. Crown 8vo, cloth extra, 7s. 6d.
HOOD'S WHIMS AND ODDITIES. With 85 Illustrations. Post 8vo, printed on laid paper and half-bound, 2s.

HOOD (TOM).—FROM NOWHERE TO THE NORTH POLE: A Noah's Arkæological Narrative. By Tom Hood. With 25 Illustrations by W. Brunton and E. C. Barnes. Square 8vo, cloth extra, gilt edges, 6s.

HOOK'S (THEODORE) CHOICE HUMOROUS WORKS; including his Ludicrous Adventures, Bons Mots, Puns, and Hoaxes. With Life of the Author, Portraits, Facsimiles, and Illustrations. Crown 8vo, cloth extra, 7s. 6d.

HOOPER.—THE HOUSE OF RABY: A Novel. By Mrs. George Hooper. Post 8vo, illustrated boards, 2s.

HOPKINS.—"'TWIXT LOVE AND DUTY:" A Novel. By Tighe Hopkins. Post 8vo, illustrated boards, 2s.

HORNE. — ORION: An Epic Poem. By Richard Hengist Horne. With Photographic Portrait by Summers. Tenth Edition. Cr. 8vo, cloth extra. 7s.

HORSE (THE) AND HIS RIDER: An Anecdotic Medley. By "Thormanby." Crown 8vo, cloth extra, 6s.

HUNT.—ESSAYS BY LEIGH HUNT: A Tale for a Chimney Corner, and other Pieces. Edited, with an Introduction, by Edmund Ollier. Post 8vo, printed on laid paper and half-bd., 2s Also in sm. sq. 8vo, cl. extra, at same price.

HUNT (MRS. ALFRED), NOVELS BY.
Crown 8vo, cloth extra, 3s. 6d. each; post 8vo, illustrated boards, 2s. each.
THE LEADEN CASKET. | SELF-CONDEMNED. | THAT OTHER PERSON.
THORNICROFT'S MODEL. Post 8vo, illustrated boards, 2s.

HYDROPHOBIA: An Account of M. Pasteur's System. Containing a Translation of all his Communications on the Subject, the Technique of his Method, and Statistics. By Renaud Suzor, M.B. Crown 8vo, cloth extra, 6s.

INGELOW (JEAN).—FATED TO BE FREE. With 24 Illustrations by G. J. Pinwell. Cr. 8vo, cloth extra, 3s. 6d.; post 8vo, illustrated boards, 2s.

INDOOR PAUPERS. By One of Them. Crown 8vo, 1s.; cloth, 1s. 6d.

IRISH WIT AND HUMOUR, SONGS OF. Collected and Edited by
A. Perceval Graves. Post 8vo, cloth limp, 2s. 6d.

JAMES.—A ROMANCE OF THE QUEEN'S HOUNDS. By Charles
James. Post 8vo, picture cover, 1s.; cloth limp, 1s. 6d.

JANVIER.—PRACTICAL KERAMICS FOR STUDENTS. By Catherine
A. Janvier. Crown 8vo, cloth extra, 6s.

JAY (HARRIETT), NOVELS BY. Post 8vo, illustrated boards, 2s. each.
THE DARK COLLEEN. | THE QUEEN OF CONNAUGHT.

JEFFERIES (RICHARD), WORKS BY. Post 8vo, cloth limp, 2s. 6d. each.
NATURE NEAR LONDON. | THE LIFE OF THE FIELDS. | THE OPEN AIR.
THE EULOGY OF RICHARD JEFFERIES. By Walter Besant. Second Edition. With a Photograph Portrait. Crown 8vo. cloth extra. 6s.

JENNINGS (H. J.), WORKS BY.
CURIOSITIES OF CRITICISM. Post 8vo, cloth limp, 2s. 6d.
LORD TENNYSON: A Biographical Sketch. With a Photograph. Cr. 8vo, cl., 6s.

JEROME. — STAGELAND : Curious Habits and Customs of its In-
habitants. By Jerome K. Jerome. With 64 Illustrations by J. Bernard Partridge.
Sixteenth Thousand. Fcap. 4to, cloth extra, 3s. 6d.

JERROLD.—THE BARBER'S CHAIR; & THE HEDGEHOG LETTERS.
By Douglas Jerrold. Post 8vo, printed on laid paper and half-bound, 2s.

JERROLD (TOM), WORKS BY. Post 8vo, 1s. each; cloth limp, 1s. 6d. each.
THE GARDEN THAT PAID THE RENT.
HOUSEHOLD HORTICULTURE. A Gossip about Flowers. Illustrated.
OUR KITCHEN GARDEN: The Plants we Grow, and How we Cook Them.

JESSE.—SCENES AND OCCUPATIONS OF A COUNTRY LIFE. By
Edward Jesse. Post 8vo, cloth limp. 2s.

JONES (WILLIAM, F.S.A.), WORKS BY. Cr. 8vo, cl. extra, 7s. 6d. each.
FINGER-RING LORE: Historical, Legendary, and Anecdotal. With nearly 300
Illustrations. Second Edition. Revised and Enlarged.
CREDULITIES, PAST AND PRESENT. Including the Sea and Seamen, Miners,
Talismans, Word and Letter Divination, Exorcising and Blessing of Animals,
Birds, Eggs, Luck, &c. With an Etched Frontispiece.
CROWNS AND CORONATIONS: A History of Regalia. With 100 Illustrations.

JONSON'S (BEN) WORKS. With Notes Critical and Explanatory
and a Biographical Memoir by William Gifford. Edited by Colonel Cunningham. Three Vols., crown 8vo, cloth extra, 6s. each.

JOSEPHUS, THE COMPLETE WORKS OF. Translated by Whiston.
Containing "The Antiquities of the Jews" and "The Wars of the Jews." With 52
Illustrations and Maps. Two Vols. demy 8vo, half-bound, 12s. 6d.

KEMPT.—PENCIL AND PALETTE : Chapters on Art and Artists. By
Robert Kempt. Post 8vo, cloth limp, 2s. 6d.

KERSHAW. — COLONIAL FACTS AND FICTIONS : Humorous
Sketches. By Mark Kershaw. Post 8vo, illustrated boards, 2s.; cloth, 2s. 6d.

KEYSER. — CUT BY THE MESS: A Novel. By Arthur Keyser.
Crown 8vo, picture cover, 1s.; cloth limp, 1s. 6d.

KING (R. ASHE), NOVELS BY. Cr. 8vo, cl., 3s. 6d. ea.; post 8vo, bds., 2s. ea.
A DRAWN GAME. | "THE WEARING OF THE GREEN."
PASSION'S SLAVE. Post 8vo, illustrated boards, 2s.
BELL BARRY. 2 vols., crown 8vo.

KINGSLEY (HENRY), NOVELS BY.
OAKSHOTT CASTLE. Post 8vo, illustrated boards, 2s.
NUMBER SEVENTEEN. Crown 8vo, cloth extra, 3s. 6d.

KNIGHTS (THE) OF THE LION : A Romance of the Thirteenth Century.
Edited, with an Introduction, by the Marquess of Lorne, K.T. Cr. 8vo, cl. ex., 6s.

KNIGHT.—THE PATIENT'S VADE MECUM: How to Get Most Benefit from Medical Advice. By WILLIAM KNIGHT, M.R.C.S., and EDWARD KNIGHT. L.R.C.P Crown 8vo, **1s.**; cloth limp, **1s. 6d.**

LAMB'S (CHARLES) COMPLETE WORKS, in Prose and Verse. Edited, with Notes and Introduction, by R. H. SHEPHERD. With Two Portraits and Facsimile of a page of the "Essay on Roast Pig." Cr. 8vo, cl. ex., **7s. 6d.**
THE ESSAYS OF ELIA. Post 8vo, printed on laid paper and half-bound, **2s.**
LITTLE ESSAYS: Sketches and Characters by CHARLES LAMB, selected from his Letters by PERCY FITZGERALD. Post 8vo, cloth limp, **2s. 6d.**

LANDOR.—CITATION AND EXAMINATION OF WILLIAM SHAKS-PEARE, &c., before Sir THOMAS LUCY, touching Deer-stealing, 19th September, 1582. To which is added, A **CONFERENCE OF MASTER EDMUND SPENSER** with the Earl of Essex, touching the State of Ireland, 1595. By WALTER SAVAGE LANDOR. Fcap. 8vo, half-Roxburghe, **2s. 6d.**

LANE.—THE THOUSAND AND ONE NIGHTS, commonly called in England THE ARABIAN NIGHTS' ENTERTAINMENTS. Translated from the Arabic, with Notes, by EDWARD WILLIAM LANE. Illustrated by many hundred Engravings from Designs by HARVEY. Edited by EDWARD STANLEY POOLE. With a Preface by STANLEY LANE-POOLE. Three Vols., demy 8vo, cloth extra, **7s. 6d.** each.

LARDER.—A SINNER'S SENTENCE: A Novel. By A. LARDER. Three Vols. Crown 8vo. [*Shortly.*

LARWOOD (JACOB), WORKS BY.
THE STORY OF THE LONDON PARKS. With Illusts. Cr. 8vo, cl. extra, **3s. 6d.**
ANECDOTES OF THE CLERGY: The Antiquities, Humours, and Eccentricities of the Cloth. Post 8vo, printed on laid paper and half-bound, **2s.**

Post 8vo, cloth limp, **2s. 6d.** each.
FORENSIC ANECDOTES. | THEATRICAL ANECDOTES.

LEIGH (HENRY S.), WORKS BY.
CAROLS OF COCKAYNE. Printed on hand-made paper, bound in buckram, **5s.**
JEUX D'ESPRIT. Edited by HENRY S. LEIGH. Post 8vo, cloth limp, **2s. 6d.**

LEYS (JOHN).—THE LINDSAYS: A Romance. Post 8vo, illust. bds., **2s.**

LIFE IN LONDON; or, The History of JERRY HAWTHORN and COR-INTHIAN TOM. With CRUIKSHANK's Coloured Illustrations. Crown 8vo, cloth extra, **7s. 6d.** [*New Edition preparing.*

LINSKILL.—IN EXCHANGE FOR A SOUL. By MARY LINSKILL. Post 8vo, illustrated boards, **2s.**

LINTON (E. LYNN), WORKS BY. Post 8vo, cloth limp, **2s. 6d.** each.
WITCH STORIES. | OURSELVES: ESSAYS ON WOMEN.

Crown 8vo, cloth extra, **3s. 6d.** each; post 8vo, illustrated boards, **2s.** each.
SOWING THE WIND. | UNDER WHICH LORD?
PATRICIA KEMBALL. | "MY LOVE!" | IONE.
ATONEMENT OF LEAM DUNDAS. | PASTON CAREW, Millionaire & Miser.
THE WORLD WELL LOST.

Post 8vo, illustrated boards, **2s.** each.
THE REBEL OF THE FAMILY. | WITH A SILKEN THREAD.

LONGFELLOW'S POETICAL WORKS. With numerous Illustrations on Steel and Wood. Crown 8vo, cloth extra, **7s. 6d.**

LUCY.—GIDEON FLEYCE: A Novel. By HENRY W. LUCY. Crown 8vo, cloth extra, **3s. 6d.**; post 8vo, illustrated boards, **2s.**

LUSIAD (THE) OF CAMOENS. Translated into English Spenserian Verse by ROBERT FFRENCH DUFF. With 14 Plates. Demy 8vo, cloth boards, **18s.**

MACALPINE (AVERY), NOVELS BY.
TERESA ITASCA, and other Stories. Crown 8vo, bound in canvas, **2s. 6d.**
BROKEN WINGS. With 6 Illusts. by W. J. HENNESSY. Crown 8vo, cloth extra, **6s.**

MACCOLL (HUGH), NOVELS BY.
MR. STRANGER'S SEALED PACKET. Second Edition. Crown 8vo, cl. extra, **5s.**
EDNOR WHITLOCK. Crown 8vo, cloth extra, **6s.**

McCARTHY (JUSTIN, M.P.), WORKS BY.

A HISTORY OF OUR OWN TIMES, from the Accession of Queen Victoria to the General Election of 1880. Four Vols. demy 8vo, cloth extra, 12s. each.—Also a POPULAR EDITION, in Four Vols., crown 8vo, cloth extra, 6s. each.—And a JUBILEE EDITION, with an Appendix of Events to the end of 1886, in Two Vols., large crown 8vo, cloth extra, 7s. 6d. each.

A SHORT HISTORY OF OUR OWN TIMES. One Vol., crown 8vo, cloth extra, 6s. —Also a CHEAP POPULAR EDITION, post 8vo, cloth limp, 2s. 6d.

A HISTORY OF THE FOUR GEORGES. Four Vols. demy 8vo, cloth extra, 12s. each. [Vols. I. & II. ready.

Crown 8vo, cloth extra, 3s. 6d. each; po . 8vo, illustrated boards, 2s. each.

THE WATERDALE NEIGHBOURS.	MISS MISANTHROPE
MY ENEMY'S DAUGHTER.	DONNA QUIXOTE.
A FAIR SAXON.	THE COMET OF A SEASON.
LINLEY ROCHFORD.	MAID OF ATHENS.
DEAR LADY DISDAIN.	CAMIOLA: A Girl with a Fortune.

"THE RIGHT HONOURABLE." By JUSTIN McCARTHY, M.P., and Mrs. CAMPBELL-PRAED. Fourth Edition. Crown 8vo, cloth extra, 6s.

McCARTHY (JUSTIN H., M.P.), WORKS BY.

THE FRENCH REVOLUTION. Four Vols., 8vo, 12s. each. [Vols. I. & II. ready.
AN OUTLINE OF THE HISTORY OF IRELAND. Crown 8vo, 1s.; cloth, 1s. 6d.
IRELAND SINCE THE UNION: Irish History, 1798-1886. Crown 8vo, cloth, 6s.
ENGLAND UNDER GLADSTONE, 1880-83. Crown 8vo, cloth extra, 6s.
HAFIZ IN LONDON: Poems. Small 8vo, gold cloth, 3s. 6d.
HARLEQUINADE: Poems. Small 4to, Japanese vellum, 8s.
OUR SENSATION NOVEL. Crown 8vo, picture cover, 1s.; cloth limp, 1s. 6d.
DOOM! An Atlantic Episode. Crown 8vo, picture cover, 1s.
DOLLY: A Sketch. Crown 8vo, picture cover, 1s.; cloth limp, 1s. 6d.
LILY LASS: A Romance. Crown 8vo, picture cover, 1s.; cloth limp, 1s. 6d.

MACDONALD (GEORGE, LL.D.), WORKS BY.

WORKS OF FANCY AND IMAGINATION. Ten Vols., cl. extra, gilt edges, in cloth case, 21s. Or the Vols. may be had separately, in grolier cl., at 2s. 6d. each.

Vol. I. WITHIN AND WITHOUT.—THE HIDDEN LIFE.
,, II. THE DISCIPLE.—THE GOSPEL WOMEN.—BOOK OF SONNETS.—ORGAN SONGS.
,, III. VIOLIN SONGS.—SONGS OF THE DAYS AND NIGHTS.—A BOOK OF DREAMS.—ROADSIDE POEMS.—POEMS FOR CHILDREN.
,, IV. PARABLES.—BALLADS.—SCOTCH SONGS.
,, V. & VI. PHANTASTES: A Faerie Romance. | Vol. VII. THE PORTENT.
,, VIII. THE LIGHT PRINCESS.—THE GIANT'S HEART.—SHADOWS.
,, IX. CROSS PURPOSES.—THE GOLDEN KEY.—THE CARASOYN.—LITTLE DAYLIGHT.
,, X. THE CRUEL PAINTER.—THE WOW O' RIVVEN.—THE CASTLE.—THE BROKEN SWORDS.—THE GRAY WOLF.—UNCLE CORNELIUS.

THE COMPLETE POETICAL WORKS OF DR. GEORGE MACDONALD. Collected and arranged by the Author. Crown 8vo, buckram, 6s. [Shortly.

MACDONELL.—QUAKER COUSINS; A Novel. By AGNES MACDONELL.

Crown 8vo, cloth extra, 3s. 6d.; post 8vo, illustrated boards, 2s.

MACGREGOR. — PASTIMES AND PLAYERS: Notes on Popular

Games. By ROBERT MACGREGOR. Post 8vo, cloth limp, 2s. 6d.

MACKAY.—INTERLUDES AND UNDERTONES; or, Music at Twilight.

By CHARLES MACKAY, LL.D. Crown 8vo, cloth extra, 6s.

MACLISE PORTRAIT GALLERY (THE) OF ILLUSTRIOUS LITER-

ARY CHARACTERS: 85 PORTRAITS; with Memoirs — Biographical, Critical, Bibliographical, and Anecdotal—illustrative of the Literature of the former half of the Present Century, by WILLIAM BATES, B.A. Crown 8vo, cloth extra, 7s. 6d.

MACQUOID (MRS.), WORKS BY. Square 8vo, cloth extra, 7s. 6d. each.

IN THE ARDENNES. With 50 Illustrations by THOMAS R. MACQUOID.
PICTURES AND LEGENDS FROM NORMANDY AND BRITTANY. With 34 Illustrations by THOMAS R. MACQUOID.
THROUGH NORMANDY. With 92 Illustrations by T. R. MACQUOID, and a Map.
THROUGH BRITTANY. With 35 Illustrations by T. R. MACQUOID, and a Map.
ABOUT YORKSHIRE. With 67 Illustrations by T. R. MACQUOID.

Post 8vo, illustrated boards, 2s. each.

THE EVIL EYE, and other Stories. | LOST ROSE.

MAGIC LANTERN, THE, and its Management: including full Practical
Directions for producing the Limelight, making Oxygen Gas, and preparing Lantern
Slides. By T. C. Hepworth. With 10 Illustrations   Cr. 8vo. 1s.; cloth. 1s. 6d.

MAGICIAN'S OWN BOOK, THE: Performances with Cups and Balls,
Eggs, Hats, Handkerchiefs, &c. All from actual Experience. Edited by W. H.
Cremer. With 200 Illustrations. Crown 8vo, cloth extra, 4s. 6d.

MAGNA CHARTA: An Exact Facsimile of the Original in the British
Museum, 3 feet by 2 feet, with Arms and Seals emblazoned in Gold and Colours, 5s.

MALLOCK (W. H.), WORKS BY.
THE NEW REPUBLIC. Post 8vo, picture cover, 2s.; cloth limp, 2s. 6d.
THE NEW PAUL & VIRGINIA: Positivism on an Island. Post 8vo, cloth, 2s. 6d.
POEMS. Small 4to, parchment, 8s.
IS LIFE WORTH LIVING? Crown 8vo, cloth extra, 6s.

MALLORY'S (SIR THOMAS) MORT D'ARTHUR: The Stories of
King Arthur and of the Knights of the Round Table. (A Selection.) Edited by B.
Montgomerie Ranking. Post 8vo, cloth limp, 2s.

MARK TWAIN, WORKS BY.   Crown 8vo, cloth extra, 7s. 6d. each.
THE CHOICE WORKS OF MARK TWAIN. Revised and Corrected throughout
   by the Author. With Life, Portrait, and numerous Illustrations.
ROUGHING IT, and INNOCENTS AT HOME. With 200 Illusts by F. A. Fraser.
THE GILDED AGE. By Mark Twain and C. D. Warner. With 212 Illustrations.
MARK TWAIN'S LIBRARY OF HUMOUR. With 197 Illustrations.
A YANKEE AT THE COURT OF KING ARTHUR. With 220 Illusts. by Beard.
THE AMERICAN CLAIMANT: The Adventures of Mulberry Sellers. With
   numerous Illustrations.   [Preparing.

Crown 8vo, cloth extra (illustrated), 7s. 6d. each; post 8vo, illust. boards, 2s. each.
THE INNOCENTS ABROAD; or New Pilgrim's Progress. With 214 Illustrations.
   (The Two-shilling Edition is entitled MARK TWAIN'S PLEASURE TRIP.)
THE ADVENTURES OF TOM SAWYER. With 111 Illustrations.
A TRAMP ABROAD. With 314 Illustrations.
THE PRINCE AND THE PAUPER. With 190 Illustrations.
LIFE ON THE MISSISSIPPI. With 300 Illustrations.
ADVENTURES OF HUCKLEBERRY FINN. With 174 Illusts. by E. W. Kemble.

THE STOLEN WHITE ELEPHANT, &c. Cr. 8vo, cl., 6s.; post 8vo, illust. bds., 2s.

MARLOWE'S WORKS. Including his Translations. Edited, with Notes
and Introductions, by Col. Cunningham. Crown 8vo, cloth extra, 6s.

MARRYAT (FLORENCE), NOVELS BY. Post 8vo, illust. boards, 2s. each.
A HARVEST OF WILD OATS. | WRITTEN IN FIRE. | FIGHTING THE AIR.
OPEN! SESAME! Crown 8vo, cloth extra, 3s. 6d.; post 8vo, picture boards, 2s.

MASSINGER'S PLAYS. From the Text of William Gifford. Edited
by Col Cunningham Crown 8vo cloth extra, 6s.

MASTERMAN.—HALF-A-DOZEN DAUGHTERS: A Novel. By J.
Masterman. Post 8vo, illustrated boards, 2s.

MATTHEWS.—A SECRET OF THE SEA, &c. By Brander Matthews.
Post 8vo, illustrated boards, 2s.; cloth limp, 2s. 6d.

MAYHEW.—LONDON CHARACTERS AND THE HUMOROUS SIDE
OF LONDON LIFE. By Henry Mayhew. With Illusts. Crown 8vo, cloth, 3s. 6d.

MENKEN.—INFELICIA: Poems by Adah Isaacs Menken. With
Biographical Preface, Illustrations by F. E. Lummis and F. O. C. Darley, and
Fac-simile of a Letter from Charles Dickens. Small 4to, cloth extra, 7s. 6d.

MEXICAN MUSTANG (ON A), through Texas to the Rio Grande. By
A. E. Sweet and J. Armoy Knox. With 265 Illusts. Cr. 8vo, cloth extra. 7s. 6d.

MIDDLEMASS (JEAN), NOVELS BY. Post 8vo, illust. boards, 2s. each.
TOUCH AND GO. | MR. DORILLION.

MILLER.—PHYSIOLOGY FOR THE YOUNG; or, The House of Life:
Human Physiology, with its application to the Preservation of Health. By Mrs.
F. Fenwick Miller. With numerous Illustrations. Post 8vo, cloth limp, 2s. 6d.

MILTON (J. L.), WORKS BY. Post 8vo, 1s. each; cloth, 1s. 6d. each.
THE HYGIENE OF THE SKIN. With Directions for Diet, Soaps, Baths, &c.
THE BATH IN DISEASES OF THE SKIN.
THE LAWS OF LIFE, AND THEIR RELATION TO DISEASES OF THE SKIN.
THE SUCCESSFUL TREATMENT OF LEPROSY. Demy 8vo, 1s.

MINTO (WM.)—WAS SHE GOOD OR BAD? Cr. 8vo, 1s. ; cloth, 1s. 6d.

MOLESWORTH (MRS.), NOVELS BY.
HATHERCOURT RECTORY. Post 8vo, illustrated boards, 2s.
THAT GIRL IN BLACK. Crown 8vo, picture cover, 1s. ; cloth, 1s. 6d.

MOORE (THOMAS), WORKS BY.
THE EPICUREAN; and ALCIPHRON. Post 8vo, half-bound, 2s.
PROSE AND VERSE, Humorous, Satirical, and Sentimental, by THOMAS MOORE;
with Suppressed Passages from the MEMOIRS OF LORD BYRON. Edited by R,
HERNE SHEPHERD. With Portrait. Crown 8vo, cloth extra, 7s. 6d.

MUDDOCK (J. E.), STORIES BY.
STORIES WEIRD AND WONDERFUL. Post 8vo, illust. boards, 2s. ; cloth, 2s. 6d.
THE DEAD MAN'S SECRET; or, The Valley of Gold: A Narrative of Strange
Adventure. With a Frontispiece by F. BARNARD. Crown 8vo, cloth extra, 5s. ;
post 8vo, illustrated boards, 2s.

MURRAY (D. CHRISTIE), NOVELS BY.
Crown 8vo, cloth extra, 3s. 6d. each; post 8vo, illustrated boards, 2s. each.

A LIFE'S ATONEMENT.	HEARTS.	A BIT OF HUMAN NATURE.
JOSEPH'S COAT.	THE WAY OF THE	FIRST PERSON SINGULAR.
COALS OF FIRE.	WORLD.	CYNIC FORTUNE.
VAL STRANGE.		

Post 8vo, picture boards, 2s. each.
A MODEL FATHER. | BY THE GATE OF THE SEA.
OLD BLAZER'S HERO. With Three Illustrations by A. McCORMICK. Crown 8vo,
cloth extra, 6s. ; post 8vo, illustrated boards. 2s.

MURRAY (D. CHRISTIE) & HENRY HERMAN, WORKS BY.
Crown 8vo, cloth extra 6s. each ; post 8vo, illustrated boards, 2s. each.
ONE TRAVELLER RETURNS.
PAUL JONES'S ALIAS. With 13 Illustrations by A. FORESTIER and G. NICOLET.
THE BISHOPS' BIBLE. Crown 8vo, cloth extra, 3s. 6d.

MURRAY.—A GAME OF BLUFF: A Novel. By HENRY MURRAY.
Post 8vo, picture boards, 2s. ; cloth limp. 2s. 6d.

NISBET (HUME), BOOKS BY.
"BAIL UP!" A Romance of BUSHRANGERS AND BLACKS. Cr 8vo, cl. ex., 3s. 6d.
LESSONS IN ART. With 21 Illustrations. Crown 8vo, cloth extra, 2s. 6d.

NOVELISTS.—HALF-HOURS WITH THE BEST NOVELISTS OF
THE CENTURY. Edit. by H. T. MACKENZIE BELL. Cr. 8vo, cl., 3s. 6d. [Preparing.

O'CONNOR. — LORD BEACONSFIELD: A Biography. By T. P.
O'CONNOR, M.P. Sixth Edition, with an Introduction. Crown 8vo, cloth extra, 5s.

O'HANLON (ALICE), NOVELS BY. Post 8vo, illustrated boards, 2s. each.
THE UNFORESEEN. | CHANCE? OR FATE?

OHNET (GEORGES), NOVELS BY.
DOCTOR RAMEAU. Translated by MRS. CASHEL HOEY. With 9 Illustrations by
E. BAYARD. Crown 8vo, cloth extra, 6s. ; post 8vo, illustrated boards, 2s.
A LAST LOVE. Translated by ALBERT D. VANDAM. Crown 8vo, cloth extra, 5s. ;
post 8vo, illustrated boards, 2s.
A WEIRD GIFT. Translated by ALBERT D. VANDAM. Crown 8vo, cloth, 3s. 6d.

OLIPHANT (MRS.), NOVELS BY. Post 8vo, illustrated boards, 2s. each.
THE PRIMROSE PATH. | THE GREATEST HEIRESS IN ENGLAND.
WHITELADIES. With Illustrations by ARTHUR HOPKINS and HENRY WOODS,
A.R.A. Crown 8vo, cloth extra, 3s. 6d. ; post 8vo, illustrated boards, 2s.

O'REILLY (MRS.). PHŒBE'S FORTUNES. Post 8vo, illust. bds. 2s.

O'SHAUGHNESSY (ARTHUR), POEMS BY.
LAYS OF FRANCE. Crown 8vo, cloth extra, 10s. 6d.
MUSIC AND MOONLIGHT. Fcap. 8vo. cloth extra, 7s. 6d.
SONGS OF A WORKER. Fcap. 8vo, cloth extra, 7s. 6d.

OUIDA, NOVELS BY. Cr. 8vo, cl., **3s. 6d.** each; post 8vo, illust. bds., **2s.** each.

HELD IN BONDAGE.	FOLLE-FARINE.	MOTHS.
TRICOTRIN.	A DOG OF FLANDERS.	PIPISTRELLO.
STRATHMORE.	PASCAREL.	A VILLAGE COMMUNE.
CHANDOS.	TWO LITTLE WOODEN	IN MAREMMA.
CECIL CASTLEMAINE'S	SHOES.	BIMBI.
GAGE.	SIGNA.	WANDA.
IDALIA.	IN A WINTER CITY.	FRESCOES. | OTHMAR.
UNDER TWO FLAGS.	ARIADNE.	PRINCESS NAPRAXINE.
PUCK.	FRIENDSHIP.	GUILDEROY. | RUFFINO.

SYRLIN. Crown 8vo, cloth extra, **3s. 6d.**
SANTA BARBARA, &c. Square 8vo, cloth extra, **6s.**

WISDOM, WIT, AND PATHOS, selected from the Works of OUIDA by F. SYDNEY MORRIS. Post 8vo, cloth extra, **5s.** CHEAP EDITION, illustrated boards, **2s.**

PAGE (H. A.), WORKS BY.
THOREAU: His Life and Aims. With Portrait. Post 8vo, cloth limp, **2s. 6d.**
ANIMAL ANECDOTES. Arranged on a New Principle. Crown 8vo, cloth extra, **5s.**

PASCAL'S PROVINCIAL LETTERS. A New Translation, with Historical Introduction and Notes by T. M'CRIE, D.D. Post 8vo, cloth limp, **2s.**

PAUL.—GENTLE AND SIMPLE. By MARGARET A. PAUL. With Frontispiece by HELEN PATERSON. Crown 8vo, cloth, **3s. 6d.**; post 8vo, illust. boards, **2s.**

PAYN (JAMES), NOVELS BY.
Crown 8vo, cloth extra, **3s. 6d.** each; post 8vo, illustrated boards, **2s.** each.

LOST SIR MASSINGBERD.	A GRAPE FROM A THORN.
WALTER'S WORD.	FROM EXILE.
LESS BLACK THAN WE'RE	SOME PRIVATE VIEWS.
PAINTED.	THE CANON'S WARD.
BY PROXY.	THE TALK OF THE TOWN.
HIGH SPIRITS.	HOLIDAY TASKS.
UNDER ONE ROOF.	GLOW-WORM TALES.
A CONFIDENTIAL AGENT.	THE MYSTERY OF MIRBRIDGE.

Post 8vo, illustrated boards, **2s.** each.

HUMOROUS STORIES.	THE CLYFFARDS OF CLYFFE.
THE FOSTER BROTHERS.	FOUND DEAD.
THE FAMILY SCAPEGRACE.	GWENDOLINE'S HARVEST.
MARRIED BENEATH HIM.	A MARINE RESIDENCE.
BENTINCK'S TUTOR.	MIRK ABBEY.
A PERFECT TREASURE.	NOT WOOED, BUT WON.
A COUNTY FAMILY.	TWO HUNDRED POUNDS REWARD.
LIKE FATHER, LIKE SON.	THE BEST OF HUSBANDS.
A WOMAN'S VENGEANCE.	HALVES. | THE BURNT MILLION.
CARLYON'S YEAR. CECIL'S TRYST.	FALLEN FORTUNES.
MURPHY'S MASTER.	WHAT HE COST HER.
AT HER MERCY.	KIT: A MEMORY. | FOR CASH ONLY.

Crown 8vo, cloth extra, **3s. 6d.** each.
IN PERIL AND PRIVATION: Stories of MARINE ADVENTURE Re-told. With 17 Illustrations.
THE WORD AND THE WILL.
SUNNY STORIES, and some SHADY ONES. With a Frontispiece by FRED. BARNARD.

NOTES FROM THE "NEWS." Crown 8vo, portrait cover, **1s.**; cloth, **1s. 6d.**

PENNELL (H. CHOLMONDELEY), WORKS BY. Post 8vo, cl., **2s. 6d.** each.
PUCK ON PEGASUS. With Illustrations.
PEGASUS RE-SADDLED. With Ten full-page Illustrations by G. DU MAURIER.
THE MUSES OF MAYFAIR. Vers de Société. Selected by H. C. PENNELL.

PHELPS (E. STUART), WORKS BY. Post 8vo, **1s.** each; cloth, **1s. 6d.** each.
BEYOND THE GATES. By the Author | AN OLD MAID'S PARADISE.
of "The Gates Ajar." | BURGLARS IN PARADISE.

JACK THE FISHERMAN. Illustrated by C. W. REED. Cr. 8vo, **1s.**; cloth, **1s. 6d.**

PIRKIS (C. L.), NOVELS BY.
TROOPING WITH CROWS. Fcap. 8vo, picture cover, **1s.**
LADY LOVELACE. Post 8vo, illustrated boards, **2s.**

PLANCHE (J. R.), WORKS BY. -
THE PURSUIVANT OF ARMS; or, Heraldry Founded upon Facts. With Coloured Frontispiece, Five Plates, and 209 Illusts. Crown 8vo, cloth, 7s. 6d.
SONGS AND POEMS, 1819-1879. Introduction by Mrs. MACKARNESS. Cr. 8vo, cl., 6s.

PLUTARCH'S LIVES OF ILLUSTRIOUS MEN. Translated from the Greek, with Notes ...itical and Historical, and a Life of Plutarch, by JOHN and WILLIAM LANGH----E. With Portraits. Two Vols., demy 8vo, half-bound, 10s. 6d.

POE'S (EDGAR ALLAN) CHOICE WORKS, in Prose and Poetry Intro-duction by CHAS. BAUDELAIRE, Portrait, and Facsimiles. Cr. 8vo, cloth, 7s. 6d.
THE MYSTERY OF MARIE ROGET, &c. Post 8vo, illustrated boards, 2s.

POPE'S POETICAL WORKS. Post 8vo, cloth limp, 2s.

PRICE (E. C.), NOVELS BY.
Crown 8vo, cloth extra, 3s. 6d. each; post 8vo, illustrated boards, 2s. each.
VALENTINA. | THE FOREIGNERS. | MRS. LANCASTER'S RIVAL.
GERALD. Post 8vo, illustrated boards, 2s.

PRINCESS OLGA.—RADNA; or, The Great Conspiracy of 1881. By
the Princess OLGA. Crown 8vo, cloth extra, 6s.

PROCTO.. (RICHARD A., B.A.), WORKS BY.
FLOWERS OF THE SKY. With 55 Illusts. Small crown 8vo, cloth extra, 3s. 6d.
EASY STAR LESSONS. With Star Maps for Every Nigh in the Year, Drawings of the Constellations, &c Crown 8vo, cloth extra, 6s.
FAMILIAR SCIENCE STUDIES. Crown 8vo, cloth extra, 6s.
SATURN AND ITS SYSTEM. With 13 Steel Plates. Demy 8vo, cloth ex., 10s. 6d.
MYSTERIES OF TIME AND SPACE. With Illustrations. Cr. 8vo, cloth extra, 6s.
THE UNIVERSE OF SUNS. With numerous Illustrations. Cr. 8vo, cloth ex., 6s.
WAGES AND WANTS OF SCIENCE WORKERS. Crown 8vo, 1s. 6d.

PRYCE.—MISS MAXWELL'S AFFECTIONS. By RICHARD PRYCE,
Author of "The Ugly Story of Miss Wetherby," &c. 2 vols., crown 8vo.

RAMBOSSON.—POPULAR ASTRONOMY. By J. RAMBOSSON, Laureate
of the Institute of France. With numerous Illusts. Crown 8vo, cloth extra, 7s. 6d.

RANDOLPH.—AUNT ABIGAIL DYKES: A Novel. By Lt.-Colonel
GEORGE RANDOLPH, U.S.A. Crown 8vo, cloth extra, 7s. 6d.

READE (CHARLES), NOVELS BY.
Crown 8vo, cloth extra, illustrated, 3s. 6d. each; post 8vo, illust. bds., 2s. each.
PEG WOFFINGTON. Illustrated by S. L. FILDES, R.A.—Also a POCKET EDITION, set in New Type, in Elzevir style, fcap. 8vo, half-leather, 2s. 6d.
CHRISTIE JOHNSTONE. Illustrated by WILLIAM SMALL.—Also a POCKET EDITION, set in New Type, in Elzevir style, fcap. 8vo, half-leather, 2s. 6d.
IT IS NEVER TOO LATE TO MEND. Illustrated by G. J. PINWELL.
THE COURSE OF TRUE LOVE NEVER DID RUN SMOOTH. Illustrated by HELEN PATERSON.
THE AUTOBIOGRAPHY OF A THIEF, &c. Illustrated by MATT STRETCH.
LOVE ME LITTLE, LOVE ME LONG. Illustrated by M. ELLEN EDWARDS.
THE DOUBLE MARRIAGE. Illusts. by Sir JOHN GILBERT, R.A., and C. KEENE.
THE CLOISTER AND THE HEARTH. Illustrated by CHARLES KEENE.
HARD CASH. Illustrated by F. W. LAWSON.
GRIFFITH GAUNT. Illustrated by S. L. FILDES, R.A., and WILLIAM SMALL.
FOUL PLAY. Illustrated by GEORGE DU MAURIER.
PUT YOURSELF IN HIS PLACE. Illustrated by ROBERT BARNES.
A TERRIBLE TEMPTATION. Illustrated by EDWARD HUGHES and A. W. COOPER.
A SIMPLETON. Illustrated by KATE CRAUFURD.
THE WANDERING HEIR. Illustrated by HELEN PATERSON, S. L. FILDES, R.A., C. GREEN, and HENRY WOODS, A.R.A.
A WOMAN-HATER. Illustrated by THOMAS COULDERY.
SINGLEHEART AND DOUBLEFACE. Illustrated by P. MACNAB.
GOOD STORIES OF MEN AND OTHER ANIMALS. Illustrated by E. A. ABBEY, PERCY MACQUOID, R.W.S., and JOSEPH NASH.
THE JILT, and other Stories. Illustrated by JOSEPH NASH.
READIANA. With a Steel-plate Portrait of CHARLES READE.
BIBLE CHARACTERS: Studies of David, Paul, &c. Fcap. 8vo, leatherette, 1s.
SELECTIONS FROM THE WORKS OF CHARLES READE. With an Introduction by Mrs. ALEX. IRELAND, and a Steel-Plate Portrait. Crown 8vo, buckram, 6s.

RIDDELL (MRS. J. H.), NOVELS BY.
Crown 8vo, cloth extra, 3s. 6d. each; post 8vo, illustrated boards, 2s. each.
HER MOTHER'S DARLING. | WEIRD STORIES.
THE PRINCE OF WALES'S GARDEN PARTY.
Post 8vo, illustrated boards, 2s. each.
UNINHABITED HOUSE. | FAIRY WATER. | MYSTERY IN PALACE GARDENS.

RIMMER (ALFRED), WORKS BY. Square 8vo, cloth gilt, 7s. 6d. each.
OUR OLD COUNTRY TOWNS. With 55 Illustrations.
RAMBLES ROUND ETON AND HARROW. With 50 Illustrations.
ABOUT ENGLAND WITH DICKENS. With 58 Illusts. by C. A. VANDERHOOF, &c.

ROBINSON CRUSOE. By DANIEL DEFOE. (MAJOR'S EDITION.) With
37 Illustrations by GEORGE CRUIKSHANK. Post 8vo, half-bound, 2s.

ROBINSON (F. W.), NOVELS BY.
Crown 8vo, cloth extra, 3s. 6d. each; post 8vo, illustrated boards, 2s. each.
WOMEN ARE STRANGE. | THE HANDS OF JUSTICE.

ROBINSON (PHIL), WORKS BY. Crown 8vo, cloth extra, 7s. 6d. each.
THE POETS' BIRDS. | THE POETS' BEASTS.
THE POETS AND NATURE: REPTILES, FISHES, INSECTS.   [Preparing.

ROCHEFOUCAULD'S MAXIMS AND MORAL REFLECTIONS. With
Notes, and an Introductory Essay by SAINTE-BEUVE. Post 8vo, cloth limp, 2s.

ROLL OF BATTLE ABBEY, THE : A List of the Principal Warriors
who came from Normandy with William the Conqueror, and Settled in this Country,
A.D. 1066-7. With Arms emblazoned in Gold and Colours. Handsomely printed, 5s.

ROWLEY (HON. HUGH), WORKS BY. Post 8vo, cloth, 2s. 6d. each.
PUNIANA: RIDDLES AND JOKES. With numerous Illustrations.
MORE PUNIANA. Profusely Illustrated.

RUNCIMAN (JAMES), STORIES BY.
Post 8vo, illustrated boards, 2s. each; cloth limp, 2s. 6d. each.
SKIPPERS AND SHELLBACKS. | GRACE BALMAIGN'S SWEETHEART.
SCHOOLS AND SCHOLARS.

RUSSELL (W. CLARK), BOOKS AND NOVELS BY :
Crown 8vo, cloth extra, 6s. each; post 8vo, illustrated boards, 2s. each.
ROUND THE GALLEY-FIRE. | A BOOK FOR THE HAMMOCK.
IN THE MIDDLE WATCH. | MYSTERY OF THE "OCEAN STAR."
A VOYAGE TO THE CAPE. | THE ROMANCE OF JENNY HARLOWE.
ON THE FO'K'SLE HEAD. Post 8vo, illustrated boards. 2s.
AN OCEAN TRAGEDY. Cr. 8vo, cloth extra, 3s. 6d.; post 8vo, illust. bds., 2s.
MY SHIPMATE LOUISE. Crown 8vo, cloth extra, 3s. 6d.

SAINT AUBYN (ALAN), NOVELS BY.
A FELLOW OF TRINITY. With a Note by OLIVER WENDELL HOLMES and a
Frontispiece. Crown 8vo, cloth extra, 3s. 6d.; post 8vo, illust. boards, 2s.
THE JUNIOR DEAN. 3 vols., crown 8vo.

SALA.—GASLIGHT AND DAYLIGHT. By GEORGE AUGUSTUS SALA.
Post 8vo, illustrated boards, 2s.

SANSON.—SEVEN GENERATIONS OF EXECUTIONERS : Memoirs
of the Sanson Family (1688 to 1847). Crown 8vo, cloth extra, 3s. 6d.

SAUNDERS (JOHN), NOVELS BY.
Crown 8vo, cloth extra, 3s. 6d. each; post 8vo, illustrated boards, 2s. each.
GUY WATERMAN. | THE LION IN THE PATH. | THE TWO DREAMERS.
BOUND TO THE WHEEL. Crown 8vo, cloth extra, 3s. 6d.

SAUNDERS (KATHARINE), NOVELS BY.
Crown 8vo, cloth extra, 3s. 6d. each; post 8vo, illustrated boards, 2s. each.
MARGARET AND ELIZABETH. | HEART SALVAGE.
THE HIGH MILLS. | SEBASTIAN.
JOAN MERRYWEATHER. Post 8vo, illustrated boards, 2s.
GIDEON'S ROCK. Crown 8vo, cloth extra, 3s. 6d.

SCIENCE-GOSSIP : An Illustrated Medium of Interchange for Students
and Lovers of Nature. Edited by Dr. J. E. TAYLOR, F.L.S., &c. Devoted to Geology,
Botany, Physiology, Chemistry, Zoology, Microscopy, Telescopy, Physiography,
Photography, &c. Price 4d. Monthly; or 5s. per year, post-free. Vols. I. to XIX.
may be had, 7s. 6d. each; Vols. XX. to date, 5s. each. Cases for Binding, 1s. 6d.

SECRET OUT, THE: One Thousand Tricks with Cards; with Enter-
taining Experiments in Drawing-room or "White Magic." By W. H. Cremer.
With 300 Illustrations. Crown 8vo, cloth extra, 4s. 6d.

SEGUIN (L. G.), WORKS BY.
THE COUNTRY OF THE PASSION PLAY (OBERAMMERGAU) and the Highlands
of Bavaria. With Map and 37 Illustrations. Crown 8vo, cloth extra, 3s. 6d.
WALKS IN ALGIERS. With 2 Maps and 16 Illusts. Crown 8vo, cloth extra, 6s.

SENIOR (WM.).—BY STREAM AND SEA. Post 8vo, cloth, 2s. 6d.

SHAKESPEARE, THE FIRST FOLIO.—Mr. William Shakespeare's
Comedies, Histories, and Tragedies. Published according to the true
Originall Copies. London, Printed by Isaac Iaggard and Ed. Blount. 1623.—
A reduced Photographic Reproduction. Small 8vo, half-Roxburghe, 7s. 6d.
SHAKESPEARE FOR CHILDREN: LAMB'S TALES FROM SHAKESPEARE. With
Illustrations, coloured and plain, by J Moyr Smith. Crown 4to, cloth, 6s.

SHARP.—CHILDREN OF TO-MORROW: A Novel. By William
Sharp. Crown 8vo, cloth extra, 6s.

SHELLEY.—THE COMPLETE WORKS IN VERSE AND PROSE OF
PERCY BYSSHE SHELLEY. Edited, Prefaced, and Annotated by R. Herne
Shepherd. Five Vols., crown 8vo, cloth boards, 3s. 6d. each.
POETICAL WORKS, in Three Vols.;
Vol. I. Introduction by the Editor; Posthumous Fragments of Margaret Nicholson; Shelley's Corre-
spondence with Stockdale; The Wandering Jew; Queen Mab, with the Notes; Alastor,
and other Poems; Rosalind and Helen; Prometheus Unbound; Adonais, &c.
Vol. II. Laon and Cythna; The Cenci; Julian and Maddalo; Swellfoot the Tyrant; The Witch of
Atlas; Epipsychidion; Hellas.
Vol. III. Posthumous Poems; The Masque of Anarchy; and other Pieces.
PROSE WORKS, in Two Vols.:
Vol. I. The Two Romances of Zastrozzi and St. Irvyne; the Dublin and Marlow Pamphlets; A Refuta-
tion of Deism; Letters to Leigh Hunt, and some Minor Writings and Fragments.
Vol. II. The Essays; Letters from Abroad; Translations and Fragments. Edited by Mrs. Shelley.
With a Bibliography of Shelley, and an Index of the Prose Works.

SHERARD.—ROGUES: A Novel. By R. H. Sherard. Crown 8vo,
picture cover, 1s.; cloth, 1s. 6d.

SHERIDAN (GENERAL). — PERSONAL MEMOIRS OF GENERAL
P. H. SHERIDAN. With Portraits and Facsimiles. Two Vols., demy 8vo, cloth, 24s.

SHERIDAN'S (RICHARD BRINSLEY) COMPLETE WORKS. With
Life and Anecdotes. Including his Dramatic Writings, his Works in Prose and
Poetry, Translations, Speeches, Jokes, &c. With 10 Illusts. Cr. 8vo, cl., 7s. 6d.
THE RIVALS, THE SCHOOL FOR SCANDAL, and other Plays. Post 8vo, printed
on laid paper and half-bound, 2s.
SHERIDAN'S COMEDIES: THE RIVALS and THE SCHOOL FOR SCANDAL.
Edited, with an Introduction and Notes to each Play, and a Biographical Sketch, by
Brander Matthews. With Illustrations. Demy 8vo, half-parchment, 12s. 6d.

SIDNEY'S (SIR PHILIP) COMPLETE POETICAL WORKS, includ-
ing all those in "Arcadia." With Portrait, Memorial-Introduction, Notes, &c. by the
Rev. A. B. Grosart, D.D. Three Vols., crown 8vo, cloth boards, 18s.

SIGNBOARDS: Their History. With Anecdotes of Famous Taverns
and Remarkable Characters. By Jacob Larwood and John Camden Hotten.
With Coloured Frontispiece and 94 Illustrations. Crown 8vo, cloth extra, 7s. 6d.

SIMS (GEORGE R.), WORKS BY.
Post 8vo, illustrated boards, 2s. each; cloth limp, 2s. 6d. each.
ROGUES AND VAGABONDS. | MARY JANE MARRIED.
THE RING O' BELLS. | TALES OF TO-DAY.
MARY JANE'S MEMOIRS. | DRAMAS OF LIFE. With 60 Illustrations.
TINKLETOP'S CRIME. With a Frontispiece by Maurice Greiffenhagen.
Crown 8vo, picture cover, 1s. each; cloth, 1s. 6d. each.
HOW THE POOR LIVE; and HORRIBLE LONDON.
THE DAGONET RECITER AND READER: being Readings and Recitations in
Prose and Verse, selected from his own Works by George R. Sims.
DAGONET DITTIES. From the Referee.
THE CASE OF GEORGE CANDLEMAS.

SISTER DORA: A Biography. By Margaret Lonsdale. With Four
Illustrations. Demy 8vo, picture cover, 4d.; cloth, 6d.

SKETCHLEY.—A MATCH IN THE DARK. By ARTHUR SKETCHLEY.
Post 8vo, illustrated boards, 2s.

SLANG DICTIONARY (THE): Etymological, Historical, and Anecdotal. Crown 8vo, cloth extra, 6s. 6d.

SMITH (J. MOYR), WORKS BY.
THE PRINCE OF ARGOLIS. With 130 Illusts. Post 8vo, cloth extra, 3s. 6d.
TALES OF OLD THULE. With numerous Illustrations. Crown 8vo, cloth gilt, 6s.
THE WOOING OF THE WATER WITCH. Illustrated. Post 8vo, cloth, 6s.

SOCIETY IN LONDON. By A FOREIGN RESIDENT. Crown 8vo, 1s.; cloth, 1s. 6d.

SOCIETY IN PARIS: The Upper Ten Thousand. A Series of Letters from Count PAUL VASILI to a Young French Diplomat. Crown 8vo, cloth, 6s.

SOMERSET. — SONGS OF ADIEU. By Lord HENRY SOMERSET. Small 4to, Japanese vellum. 6s.

SPALDING.—ELIZABETHAN DEMONOLOGY: An Essay on the Belief in the Existence of Devils. By T. A. SPALDING, LL.B. Crown 8vo, cloth extra, 5s.

SPEIGHT (T. W.), NOVELS BY.
Post 8vo, illustrated boards. 2s. each.

THE MYSTERIES OF HERON DYKE.	THE GOLDEN HOOP.
BY DEVIOUS WAYS, and A BARREN TITLE.	HOODWINKED; and THE SANDYCROFT MYSTERY.

Post 8vo, cloth limp, 1s. 6d. each.

A BARREN TITLE.	WIFE OR NO WIFE?

THE SANDYCROFT MYSTERY. Crown 8vo, picture cover, 1s.

SPENSER FOR CHILDREN. By M. H. TOWRY. With Illustrations by WALTER J. MORGAN. Crown 4to, cloth gilt, 6s.

STARRY HEAVENS (THE): A POETICAL BIRTHDAY BOOK. Royal 16mo, cloth extra, 2s. 6d.

STAUNTON.—THE LAWS AND PRACTICE OF CHESS. With an Analysis of the Openings. By HOWARD STAUNTON. Edited by ROBERT B. WORMALD. Crown 8vo, cloth extra. 5s.

STEDMAN (E. C.), WORKS BY.
VICTORIAN POETS. Thirteenth Edition. Crown 8vo. cloth extra, 9s.
THE POETS OF AMERICA. Crown 8vo, cloth extra. 9s.

STERNDALE. — THE AFGHAN KNIFE: A Novel. By ROBERT ARMITAGE STERNDALE. Cr. 8vo, cloth extra. 3s. 6d.; post 8vo, illust. boards 2s.

STEVENSON (R. LOUIS), WORKS BY. Post 8vo, cl. limp, 2s. 6d. each.
TRAVELS WITH A DONKEY. Eighth Edit. With a Frontis. by WALTER CRANE.
AN INLAND VOYAGE. Fourth Edition. With a Frontispiece by WALTER CRANE.

Crown 8vo, buckram, gilt top, 6s. each.
FAMILIAR STUDIES OF MEN AND BOOKS. Fifth Edition.
THE SILVERADO SQUATTERS. With a Frontispiece. Third Edition.
THE MERRY MEN. Second Edition. | UNDERWOODS: Poems. Fifth Edition.
MEMORIES AND PORTRAITS. Third Edition.
VIRGINIBUS PUERISQUE, and other Papers. Fifth Edition. | BALLADS.

NEW ARABIAN NIGHTS. Eleventh Edition. Crown 8vo, buckram, gilt top, 6s.; post 8vo, illustrated boards, 2s.
PRINCE OTTO. Post 8vo, illustrated boards, 2s.
FATHER DAMIEN: An Open Letter to the Rev. Dr. Hyde. Second Edition. Crown 8vo, hand-made and brown paper, 1s.

STODDARD. — SUMMER CRUISING IN THE SOUTH SEAS. By C. WARREN STODDARD. Illustrated by WALLIS MACKAY. Cr. 8vo, cl. extra, 3s. 6d.

STORIES FROM FOREIGN NOVELISTS. With Notices by HELEN and ALICE ZIMMERN. Crown 8vo, cloth extra, 3s. 6d.; post 8vo, illustrated boards, 2s.

STRANGE MANUSCRIPT (A) FOUND IN A COPPER CYLINDER. With 19 Illustrations by GILBERT GAUL. Third Edition. Crown 8vo, cloth extra, 5s.

STRUTT'S SPORTS AND PASTIMES OF THE PEOPLE OF ENGLAND; including the Rural and Domestic Recreations, May Games, Mummeries, Shows, &c., from the Earliest Period to the Present Time. Edited by WILLIAM HONE. With 140 Illustrations. Crown 8vo, cloth extra, 7s. 6d.

SUBURBAN HOMES (THE) OF LONDON : A Residential Guide. With a Map, and Notes on Rental, Rates, and Accommodation. Crown 8vo, cloth, 7s. 6d.

SWIFT'S (DEAN) CHOICE WORKS, in Prose and Verse. With Memoir, Portrait, and Facsimiles of the Maps in "Gulliver's Travels." Cr. 8vo, cl., 7s. 6d.

GULLIVER'S TRAVELS, and **A TALE OF A TUB.** Post 8vo, printed on laid paper and half-bound, 2s.

A MONOGRAPH ON SWIFT. By J. CHURTON COLLINS. Cr. 8vo, cloth, 8s. [Shortly.

SWINBURNE (ALGERNON C.), WORKS BY.

SELECTIONS FROM POETICAL WORKS OF A. C. SWINBURNE. Fcap. 8vo, 6s.
ATALANTA IN CALYDON. Cr. 8vo, 6s.
CHASTELARD : A Tragedy. Cr. 8vo. 7s.
NOTES ON POEMS AND REVIEWS. Demy 8vo, 1s.
POEMS AND BALLADS. FIRST SERIES. Crown 8vo or fcap. 8vo, 9s.
POEMS AND BALLADS. SECOND SERIES. Crown 8vo or fcap. 8vo, 9s.
POEMS AND BALLADS. THIRD SERIES. Crown 8vo. 7s.
SONGS BEFORE SUNRISE. Crown 8vo, 10s. 6d.
BOTHWELL : A Tragedy. Crown 8vo, 12s. 6d.
SONGS OF TWO NATIONS. Cr. 8vo, 6s.

GEORGE CHAPMAN. (See Vol. II. of G. CHAPMAN'S Works.) Crown 8vo, 6s.
ESSAYS AND STUDIES. Cr. 8vo, 12s.
ERECHTHEUS : A Tragedy. Cr. 8vo, 6s.
SONGS OF THE SPRINGTIDES. Crown 8vo. 6s.
STUDIES IN SONG. Crown 8vo, 7s.
MARY STUART : A Tragedy. Cr. 8vo 8s
TRISTRAM OF LYONESSE. Cr. 8vo, 9s.
A CENTURY OF ROUNDELS. Sm. 4to, 8s.
A MIDSUMMER HOLIDAY. Cr. 8vo, 7s.
MARINO FALIERO : A Tragedy. Crown 8vo. 6s.
A STUDY OF VICTOR HUGO. Cr. 8vo, 6s.
MISCELLANIES. Crown 8vo, 12s.
LOCRINE : A Tragedy. Cr. 8vo, 6s.
A STUDY OF BEN JONSON. Cr. 8vo, 7s.

SYMONDS.—WINE, WOMEN, AND SONG : Mediæval Latin Students' Songs. With Essay and Trans. by J. ADDINGTON SYMONDS. Fcap. 8vo, parchment, 6s.

SYNTAX'S (DR.) THREE TOURS : In Search of the Picturesque, in Search of Consolation, and in Search of a Wife. With ROWLANDSON'S Coloured Illustrations, and Life of the Author by J. C. HOTTEN. Crown 8vo, cloth extra, 7s. 6d.

TAINE'S HISTORY OF ENGLISH LITERATURE. Translated by HENRY VAN LAUN. Four Vols., medium 8vo, cloth boards, 30s.—POPULAR EDITION, Two Vols., large crown 8vo, cloth extra, 15s.

TAYLOR'S (BAYARD) DIVERSIONS OF THE ECHO CLUB : Burlesques of Modern Writers. Post 8vo, cloth limp, 2s.

TAYLOR (DR. J. E., F.L.S.), WORKS BY. Cr. 8vo, cl. ex., 7s. 6d. each.

THE **SAGACITY** AND MORALITY OF PLANTS : A Sketch of the Life and Conduct of the Vegetable Kingdom. With a Coloured Frontispiece and 100 Illustrations.

OUR COMMON BRITISH FOSSILS, and Where to Find Them. 331 Illustrations.

THE PLAYTIME NATURALIST. With 366 Illustrations. Crown 8vo, cloth, 5s.

TAYLOR'S (TOM) HISTORICAL DRAMAS. Containing "Clancarty," "Jeanne Darc," "'Twixt Axe and Crown," "The Fool's Revenge," "Arkwright's Wife," "Anne Boleyn," " Plot and Passion." Crown 8vo, cloth extra, 7s. 6d.
. The Plays may also be had separately, at 1s. each.

TENNYSON (LORD) : A Biographical Sketch. By H. J. JENNINGS. With a Photograph-Portrait. Crown 8vo, cloth extra, 6s.

THACKERAYANA : Notes and Anecdotes. Illustrated by Hundreds of Sketches by WILLIAM MAKEPEACE THACKERAY, depicting Humorous Incidents in his School-life, and Favourite Characters in the Books of his Every-day Reading. With a Coloured Frontispiece. Crown 8vo, cloth extra, 7s. 6d.

THAMES.—A NEW PICTORIAL HISTORY OF THE THAMES. By A. S. KRAUSSE. With 340 Illustrations. Post 8vo, 1s.; cloth, 1s. 6d.

THOMAS (BERTHA), NOVELS BY. Cr. 8vo, cl., 3s. 6d. ea.; post 8vo, 2s. ea.
CRESSIDA. | THE VIOLIN-PLAYER. | PROUD MAISIE.

THOMSON'S SEASONS, and CASTLE OF INDOLENCE. Introduction
by ALLAN CUNNINGHAM, and Illustrations on Steel and Wood. Cr. 8vo, cl., 7s. 6d.

THORNBURY (WALTER), WORKS BY. Cr. 8vo, cl. extra, 7s. 6d. each.
THE LIFE AND CORRESPONDENCE OF J. M. W. TURNER. Founded upon
Letters and Papers furnished by his Friends. With Illustrations in Colours.
HAUNTED LONDON. Edit. by E. WALFORD, M.A. Illusts. by F. W. FAIRHOLT, F.S.A.

Post 8vo, illustrated boards, 2s. each.
OLD STORIES RE-TOLD. | TALES FOR THE MARINES.

TIMBS (JOHN), WORKS BY. Crown 8vo, cloth extra, 7s. 6d. each.
THE HISTORY OF CLUBS AND CLUB LIFE IN LONDON: Anecdotes of its
Famous Coffee-houses, Hostelries, and Taverns. With 42 Illustrations.
ENGLISH ECCENTRICS AND ECCENTRICITIES: Stories of Wealth and Fashion,
Delusions, Impostures, and Fanatic Missions, Sporting Scenes, Eccentric Artists,
Theatrical Folk, Men of Letters, &c. With 48 Illustrations.

TROLLOPE (ANTHONY), NOVELS BY.
Crown 8vo, cloth extra, 3s. 6d. each; post 8vo, illustrated boards, 2s. each.
THE WAY WE LIVE NOW. | MARION FAY.
KEPT IN THE DARK. | MR. SCARBOROUGH'S FAMILY.
FRAU FROHMANN. | THE LAND-LEAGUERS.

Post 8vo, illustrated boards, 2s. each.
GOLDEN LION OF GRANPERE. | JOHN CALDIGATE. | AMERICAN SENATOR.

TROLLOPE (FRANCES E.), NOVELS BY.
Crown 8vo, cloth extra, 3s. 6d. each; post 8vo, illustrated boards, 2s. each.
LIKE SHIPS UPON THE SEA. | MABEL'S PROGRESS. | ANNE FURNESS.

TROLLOPE (T. A.).—DIAMOND CUT DIAMOND. Post 8vo, illust. bds., 2s.

TROWBRIDGE.—FARNELL'S FOLLY: A Novel.   By J. T. TROW-
BRIDGE. Post 8vo, illustrated boards 2s.

TYTLER (C. C. FRASER-).—MISTRESS JUDITH: A Novel.   By
C. C. FRASER-TYTLER. Crown 8vo, cloth extra, 3s. 6d.; post 8vo, illust. boards, 2s.

TYTLER (SARAH), NOVELS BY.
Crown 8vo, cloth extra, 3s. 6d. each; post 8vo, illustrated boards, 2s. each.
THE BRIDE'S PASS. | BURIED DIAMONDS.
NOBLESSE OBLIGE. | THE BLACKHALL GHOSTS.
LADY BELL.

Post 8vo, illustrated boards, 2s. each.
WHAT SHE CAME THROUGH. | BEAUTY AND THE BEAST.
CITOYENNE JACQUELINE. | DISAPPEARED.
SAINT MUNGO'S CITY. | THE HUGUENOT FAMILY.

VILLARI.—A DOUBLE BOND. By LINDA VILLARI. Fcap. 8vo, picture
cover 1s.

WALT WHITMAN, POEMS BY. Edited, with Introduction, by
WILLIAM M. ROSSETTI. With Portrait. Cr. 8vo, hand-made paper and buckram, 6s.

WALTON AND COTTON'S COMPLETE ANGLER; or, The Con-
templative Man's Recreation, by IZAAK WALTON; and Instructions how to Angle for a
Trout or Grayling in a clear Stream, by CHARLES COTTON. With Memoirs and Notes
by Sir HARRIS NICOLAS, and 61 Illustrations. Crown 8vo, cloth antique, 7s. 6d.

WARD (HERBERT), WORKS BY.
FIVE YEARS WITH THE CONGO CANNIBALS. With 92 Illustrations by the
Author, VICTOR PERARD, and W. B. DAVIS. Third ed. Roy. 8vo, cloth ex., 14s.
MY LIFE WITH STANLEY'S REAR GUARD. With a Map by F. S. WELLER,
F.R.G.S. Post 8vo, 1s.; cloth, 1s. 6d.

WARNER.—A ROUNDABOUT JOURNEY. By CHARLES DUDLEY
WARNER. Crown 8vo, cloth extra, 6s.

WALFORD (EDWARD, M.A.), WORKS BY.

WALFORD'S COUNTY FAMILIES OF THE UNITED KINGDOM (1891). Containing the Descent, Birth, Marriage, Education, &c., of 12,000 Heads of Families, their Heirs. Offices, Addresses, Clubs, &c. Royal 8vo, cloth gilt, **50s.**

WALFORD'S SHILLING PEERAGE (1891). Containing a List of the House of Lords, Scotch and Irish Peers, &c. 32mo. cloth, **1s.**

WALFORD'S SHILLING BARONETAGE (1891). Containing a List of the Baronets of the United Kingdom, Biographical Notices, Addresses, &c. 32mo, cloth, **1s.**

WALFORD'S SHILLING KNIGHTAGE (1891). Containing a List of the Knights of the United Kingdom, Biographical Notices, Addresses, &c. 32mo, cloth, **1s.**

WALFORD'S SHILLING HOUSE OF COMMONS (1891). Containing a List of all Members of Parliament, their Addresses, Clubs, &c. 32mo, cloth, **1s.**

WALFORD'S COMPLETE PEERAGE, **BARONETAGE, KNIGHTAGE, AND** HOUSE OF COMMONS (1891). Royal 32mo, cloth extra, gilt edges, **5s.**

WALFORD'S WINDSOR PEERAGE, **BARONETAGE, AND KNIGHTAGE** (1891). Crown 8vo, cloth extra, **12s. 6d.**

TALES OF OUR GREAT FAMILIES. Crown 8vo, cloth extra, **3s. 6d.**

WILLIAM PITT: A Biography. Post 8vo, cloth extra, **5s.**

WARRANT TO EXECUTE CHARLES I. A Facsimile, with the 59 Signatures and Seals. Printed on paper 22 in. by 14 in. **2s.**

WARRANT **TO EXECUTE** MARY QUEEN OF SCOTS. A Facsimile, including Queen Elizabeth's Signature and the Great Seal. **2s.**

WEATHER, HOW TO FORETELL THE, WITH POCKET SPEC-TROSCOPE. By F. W. Cory. With 10 Illustrations. Cr. 8vo. **1s.**; cloth, **1s. 6d.**

WESTROPP.—HANDBOOK OF POTTERY AND PORCELAIN. By HODDER M. WESTROPP. With Illusts. and List of Marks. Cr. 8vo. cloth, **4s. 6d.**

WHIST.—HOW TO PLAY SOLO WHIST. By ABRAHAM S. WILKS and CHARLES F. PARDON. Crown 8vo, cloth extra, **3s. 6d.**

WHISTLER'S (MR.) TEN O'CLOCK. Cr. 8vo, hand-made paper, 1s.

WHITE.—THE NATURAL HISTORY OF SELBORNE. By GILBERT WHITE, M.A. Post 8vo, printed on laid paper and half-bound, **2s.**

WILLIAMS (W. MATTIEU, F.R.A.S.), WORKS BY.

SCIENCE IN SHORT CHAPTERS. Crown 8vo, cloth extra, **7s. 6d.**

A SIMPLE TREATISE ON HEAT. With Illusts. Cr. 8vo, cloth limp, **2s. 6d.**

THE CHEMISTRY OF COOKERY. Crown 8vo, cloth extra, **6s.**

THE CHEMISTRY OF IRON AND STEEL MAKING. Crown 8vo, cloth extra, **9s.**

WILLIAMSON.—A CHILD WIDOW. By Mrs. F. H. WILLIAMSON. Three Vols., crown 8vo.

WILSON (DR. ANDREW, F.R.S.E.), WORKS BY.

CHAPTERS ON EVOLUTION. With 259 Illustrations. Cr. 8vo, cloth extra, **7s. 6d.**

LEAVES FROM A NATURALIST'S NOTE-BOOK. Post 8vo, cloth limp, **2s. 6d.**

LEISURE-TIME STUDIES. With Illustrations. Crown 8vo, cloth extra, **6s.**

STUDIES IN LIFE AND SENSE. With numerous Illusts. Cr. 8vo, cl. ex., **6s.**

COMMON ACCIDENTS: HOW TO TREAT THEM. Illusts. Cr. 8vo, **1s.**; cl., **1s. 6d.**

GLIMPSES OF NATURE. With 35 Illustrations. Crown 8vo, cloth extra, **3s. 6d.**

WINTER (J. S.), STORIES BY. Post 8vo, illustrated boards, **2s.** each.

CAVALRY LIFE. | REGIMENTAL LEGENDS.

WISSMANN.—MY SECOND JOURNEY THROUGH EQUATORIAL AFRICA, from the Congo to the Zambesi, in 1886, 1887. By Major HERMANN VON WISSMANN. Trans. by M. J. A. BERGMANN. Map by F. S. WELLER and 92 Illusts. by R. HELLGREWE and KLEIN-CHEVALIER. Demy 8vo, cloth extra, **16s.** [Shortly.

WOOD.—SABINA: A Novel. By Lady WOOD. Post 8vo, boards, 2s.

WOOD (H. F.), DETECTIVE STORIES BY.

Crown 8vo, cloth extra, **6s.** each; post 8vo, illustrated boards, **2s.** each.

PASSENGER **FROM** SCOTLAND YARD. | ENGLISHMAN OF THE RUE CAIN.

WOOLLEY.—RACHEL ARMSTRONG; or, Love and Theology. By CELIA PARKER WOOLLEY. Post 8vo, illustrated boards, **2s.**; cloth, **2s. 6d.**

WRIGHT (THOMAS), WORKS BY. Crown 8vo, cloth extra, **7s. 6d.** each.

CARICATURE HISTORY OF THE GEORGES. With 400 Pictures, Caricatures, Squibs, Broadsides, Window Pictures, &c.

HISTORY OF CARICATURE AND OF THE GROTESQUE IN ART, LITERATURE, SCULPTURE, AND PAINTING. Illustrated by F. W. FAIRHOLT, F.S.A.

YATES (EDMUND), NOVELS BY. Post 8vo, illustrated boards, **2s.** each.

LAND AT LAST. | THE **FORLORN HOPE.** | **CASTAWAY.**

LISTS OF BOOKS CLASSIFIED IN SERIES.

, *For fuller cataloguing, see alphabetical arrangement, pp. 1-25.*

THE MAYFAIR LIBRARY. Post 8vo, cloth limp, 2s. 6d. per Volume.

A Journey Round My Room. By XAVIER DE MAISTRE.
Quips and Quiddities. By W. D. ADAMS.
The Agony Column of "The Times."
Melancholy Anatomised: Abridgment of "Burton's Anatomy of Melancholy."
The Speeches of Charles Dickens.
Literary Frivolities, Fancies, Follies, and Frolics. By W. T. DOBSON.
Poetical Ingenuities. By W. T. DOBSON.
The Cupboard Papers. By FIN-BEC.
W. S. Gilbert's Plays. FIRST SERIES.
W. S. Gilbert's Plays. SECOND SERIES.
Songs of Irish Wit and Humour.
Animals and Masters. By Sir A. HELPS.
Social Pressure. By Sir A. HELPS.
Curiosities of Criticism. H. J. JENNINGS.
Holmes's Autocrat of Breakfast-Table.
Pencil and Palette. By R. KEMPT.

Little Essays: from LAMB's Letters.
Forensic Anecdotes. By JACOB LARWOOD.
Theatrical Anecdotes. JACOB LARWOOD.
Jeux d'Esprit. Edited by HENRY S. LEIGH.
Witch Stories. By E. LYNN LINTON.
Ourselves. By E. LYNN LINTON.
Pastimes & Players. By R. MACGREGOR.
New Paul and Virginia. W.H.MALLOCK.
New Republic. By W. H. MALLOCK.
Puck on Pegasus. By H. C. PENNELL.
Pegasus Re-Saddled. By H. C. PENNELL.
Muses of Mayfair. Ed. H. C. PENNELL.
Thoreau: His Life & Aims. By H. A. PAGE.
Puniana. By Hon. HUGH ROWLEY.
More Puniana. By Hon. HUGH ROWLEY.
The Philosophy of Handwriting.
By Stream and Sea. By WM. SENIOR.
Leaves from a Naturalist's Note-Book. By Dr. ANDREW WILSON.

THE GOLDEN LIBRARY. Post 8vo, cloth limp, 2s. per Volume.

Bayard Taylor's Diversions of the Echo Club.
Bennett's Ballad History of England.
Bennett's Songs for Sailors.
Godwin's Lives of the Necromancers.
Pope's Poetical Works.
Holmes's Autocrat of Breakfast Table.

Holmes's Professor at Breakfast Table.
Jesse's Scenes of Country Life.
Leigh Hunt's Tale for a Chimney Corner.
Mallory's Mort d'Arthur: Selections.
Pascal's Provincial Letters.
Rochefoucauld's Maxims & Reflections.

THE WANDERER'S LIBRARY. Crown 8vo, cloth extra, 3s. 6d. each.

Wanderings in Patagonia. By JULIUS BEERBOHM. Illustrated.
Camp Notes. By FREDERICK BOYLE.
Savage Life. By FREDERICK BOYLE.
Merrie England in the Olden Time. By G. DANIEL. Illustrated by CRUIKSHANK.
Circus Life. By THOMAS FROST.
Lives of the Conjurers. THOMAS FROST.
The Old Showmen and the Old London Fairs. By THOMAS FROST.
Low-Life Deeps. By JAMES GREENWOOD.

Wilds of London. JAMES GREENWOOD.
Tunis. Chev. HESSE-WARTEGG. 22 Illusts.
Life and Adventures of a Cheap Jack.
World Behind the Scenes. P. FITZGERALD.
Tavern Anecdotes and Sayings.
The Genial Showman. By E.P. HINGSTON.
Story of London Parks. JACOB LARWOOD.
London Characters. By HENRY MAYHEW.
Seven Generations of Executioners.
Summer Cruising in the South Seas. By C. WARREN STODDARD. Illustrated.

POPULAR SHILLING BOOKS.

Harry Fludyer at Cambridge.
Jeff Briggs's Love Story. BRET HARTE.
Twins of Table Mountain. BRET HARTE.
A Day's Tour. By PERCY FITZGERALD.
Esther's Glove. By R. E. FRANCILLON.
Sentenced! By SOMERVILLE GIBNEY.
The Professor's Wife. By L. GRAHAM.
Mrs. Gainsborough's Diamonds. By JULIAN HAWTHORNE.
Niagara Spray. By J. HOLLINGSHEAD.
A Romance of the Queen's Hounds. By CHARLES JAMES.
The Garden that Paid the Rent. By TOM JERROLD.
Cut by the Mess. By ARTHUR KEYSER.
Our Sensation Novel. J. H. McCARTHY.
Doom! By JUSTIN H. McCARTHY, M.P.
Dolly. By JUSTIN H. McCARTHY, M.P.
Lily Lass. JUSTIN H. McCARTHY, M.P.

Was She Good or Bad? By W. MINTO.
That Girl in Black. Mrs. MOLESWORTH.
Notes from the "News." By JAS. PAYN.
Beyond the Gates. By E. S. PHELPS.
Old Maid's Paradise. By E. S. PHELPS.
Burglars in Paradise. By E. S. PHELPS.
Jack the Fisherman. By E. S. PHELPS.
Trooping with Crows. By C. L. PIRKIS.
Bible Characters. By CHARLES READE.
Rogues. By R. H. SHERARD.
The Dagonet Reciter. By G. R. SIMS.
How the Poor Live. By G. R. SIMS.
Case of George Candlemas. G. R. SIMS.
Sandycroft Mystery. T. W. SPEIGHT.
Hoodwinked. By T. W. SPEIGHT.
Father Damien. By R. L. STEVENSON.
A Double Bond. By LINDA VILLARI.
My Life with Stanley's Rear Guard. By HERBERT WARD.

MY LIBRARY.

Choice Works, printed on laid paper, bound half-Roxburghe, **2s. 6d.** each.

Four Frenchwomen. By Austin Dobson.
Citation and Examination of William Shakspeare. By W. S. Landor.
Christie Johnstone. By Charles Reade. With a Photogravure Frontispiece.
Peg Woffington. By Charles Reade.
The Journal of Maurice de Guerin.

THE POCKET LIBRARY. Post 8vo, printed on laid paper and hf.-bd., 2s. each.

The Essays of Elia. By Charles Lamb.
Robinson Crusoe. Edited by John Major. With 37 Illusts. by George Cruikshank.
Whims and Oddities. By Thomas Hood. With 85 Illustrations.
The Barber's Chair, and **The Hedgehog Letters.** By Douglas Jerrold.
Gastronomy as a Fine Art. By Brillat-Savarin. Trans. R. E. Anderson, M.A.
The Epicurean, &c. By Thomas Moore.
Leigh Hunt's Essays. Ed. E. Ollier.
The Natural History of Selborne. By Gilbert White.
Gulliver's Travels, and The Tale of a Tub. By Dean Swift.
The Rivals, School for Scandal, and other Plays by Richard Brinsley Sheridan.
Anecdotes of the Clergy. J. Larwood.

THE PICCADILLY NOVELS.

Library Editions of Novels by the Best Authors, many Illustrated, crown 8vo, cloth extra, 3s. 6d. each.

By GRANT ALLEN.
Philistia.
Babylon.
In all Shades.
The Tents of Shem.
For Mamie's Sake.
The Devil's Die.
This Mortal Coil.
The Great Taboo.

By ALAN ST. AUBYN.
A Fellow of Trinity.

By Rev. S. BARING GOULD.
Red Spider. | Eve.

By W. BESANT & J. RICE.
My Little Girl.
Case of Mr. Lucraft.
This Son of Vulcan.
Golden Butterfly.
Ready-Money Mortiboy.
With Harp and Crown.
'Twas in Trafalgar's Bay.
The Chaplain of the Fleet.
By Celia's Arbour.
Monks of Thelema.
The Seamy Side.
Ten Years' Tenant.

By WALTER BESANT.
All Sorts and Conditions of Men.
The Captains' Room.
All in a Garden Fair
The World Went Very Well Then.
For Faith and Freedom.
Dorothy Forster.
Uncle Jack.
Children of Gibeon.
Herr Paulus.
Bell of St. Paul's.
To Call Her Mine.
The Holy Rose.
Armorel of Lyonesse.

By ROBERT BUCHANAN.
The Shadow of the Sword.
A Child of Nature.
The Martyrdom of Madeline.
God and the Man.
Love Me for Ever.
Annan Water.
Matt.
The New Abelard.
Foxglove Manor.
Master of the Mine.
Heir of Linne.

By HALL CAINE.
The Shadow of a Crime.
A Son of Hagar. | The Deemster.

MORT. & FRANCES COLLINS.
Sweet Anne Page. | Transmigration.
From Midnight to Midnight.
Blacksmith and Scholar.
Village Comedy. | You Play Me False

By Mrs. H. LOVETT CAMERON.
Juliet's Guardian. | Deceivers Ever.

By WILKIE COLLINS.
Armadale.
After Dark.
No Name.
Antonina. | Basil.
Hide and Seek.
The Dead Secret.
Queen of Hearts.
My Miscellanies.
Woman in White.
The Moonstone.
Man and Wife.
Poor Miss Finch.
Miss or Mrs?
New Magdalen.
The Frozen Deep.
The Two Destinies.
Law and the Lady.
Haunted Hotel.
The Fallen Leaves.
Jezebel's Daughter
The Black Robe.
Heart and Science.
"I Say No."
Little Novels.
The Evil Genius.
The Legacy of Cain
A Rogue's Life.
Blind Love.

By DUTTON COOK.
Paul Foster's Daughter.

By WILLIAM CYPLES.
Hearts of Gold.

By ALPHONSE DAUDET.
The Evangelist; or, Port Salvation.

By JAMES DE MILLE.
A Castle in Spain.

By J. LEITH DERWENT.
Our Lady of Tears. | Circe's Lovers.

By Mrs. ANNIE EDWARDES.
Archie Lovell.

By G. MANVILLE FENN.
The New Mistress.

By PERCY FITZGERALD.
Fatal Zero.

By R. E. FRANCILLON.
Queen Cophetua.
One by One.
A Real Queen.
King or Knave?

Pref. by Sir BARTLE FRERE.
Pandurang Hari.

By EDWARD GARRETT.
The Capel Girls.

By CHARLES GIBBON.
Robin Gray. | The Golden Shaft.
In Honour Bound. | Of High Degree.
Loving a Dream.
The Flower of the Forest.

By JULIAN HAWTHORNE.
Garth. | Dust.
Ellice Quentin. | Fortune's Fool.
Sebastian Strome. | Beatrix Randolph.
David Poindexter's Disappearance.
The Spectre of the Camera.

By Sir A. HELPS.
Ivan de Biron.

By ISAAC HENDERSON.
Agatha Page.

By Mrs. ALFRED HUNT.
The Leaden Casket. | Self-Condemned.
That other Person.

By JEAN INGELOW
Fated to be Free.

By R. ASHE KING.
A Drawn Game.
"The Wearing of the Green."

By HENRY KINGSLEY.
Number Seventeen.

By E. LYNN LINTON.
Patricia Kemball. | Ione.
Under which Lord? | Paston Carew.
"My Love!" | Sowing the Wind.
The Atonement of Leam Dundas.
The World Well Lost.

By HENRY W. LUCY.
Gideon Fleyce.

By JUSTIN McCARTHY.
A Fair Saxon. | Donna Quixote.
Linley Rochford. | Maid of Athens.
Miss Misanthrope. | Camiola.
The Waterdale Neighbours.
My Enemy's Daughter.
Dear Lady Disdain.
The Comet of a Season.

By AGNES MACDONELL.
Quaker Cousins.

By FLORENCE MARRYAT.
Open! Sesame!

By D. CHRISTIE MURRAY.
Life's Atonement. | Val Strange.
Joseph's Coat. | Hearts.
Coals of Fire.
A Bit of Human Nature.
First Person Singular.
Cynic Fortune.
The Way of the World.

By MURRAY & HERMAN.
The Bishops' Bible.

By GEORGES OHNET.
A Weird Gift.

By Mrs. OLIPHANT.
Whiteladies.

By OUIDA.
Held in Bondage. | Two Little Wooden
Strathmore. | Shoes.
Chandos. | In a Winter City.
Under Two Flags. | Ariadne.
Idalia. | Friendship.
CecilCastlemaine's | Moths. | Ruffino.
Gage. | Pipistrello.
Tricotrin. | Puck. | A Village Commune
Folle Farine. | Bimbi. | Wanda.
A Dog of Flanders. | Frescoes.
Pascarel. | Signa. | In Maremma.
Princess Naprax- | Othmar. | Syrlin.
ine. | Guilderoy.

By MARGARET A. PAUL.
Gentle and Simple.

By JAMES PAYN.
Lost Sir Massingberd.
Less Black than We're Painted.
A Confidential Agent.
A Grape from a Thorn.
Some Private Views.
In Peril and Privation.
The Mystery of Mirbridge.
The Canon's Ward.
Walter's Word. | Talk of the Town.
By Proxy. | Holiday Tasks.
High Spirits. | The Burnt Million.
Under One Roof. | The Word and the
From Exile. | Will.
Glow-worm Tales. | Sunny Stories.

By E. C. PRICE.
Valentina. | The Foreigners.
Mrs. Lancaster's Rival.

By CHARLES READE.
It is Never Too Late to Mend.
The Double Marriage.
Love Me Little, Love Me Long.
The Cloister and the Hearth.
The Course of True Love.
The Autobiography of a Thief.
Put Yourself in his Place.
A Terrible Temptation.
Singleheart and Doubleface.
Good Stories of Men and other Animals.
Hard Cash. | Wandering Heir.
Peg Woffington. | A Woman-Hater
Christie Johnstone. | A Simpleton.
Griffith Gaunt. | Readiana.
Foul Play. | The Jilt.

By Mrs. J. H. RIDDELL.
Her Mother's Darling.
Prince of Wales's Garden Party.
Weird Stories.

By F. W. ROBINSON.
Women are Strange.
The Hands of Justice.

By W. CLARK RUSSELL.
An Ocean Tragedy.
My Shipmate Louise.

By JOHN SAUNDERS.
Guy Waterman. | Two Dreamers.
Bound to the Wheel.
The Lion in the Path.

Two-Shilling Novels—*continued.*

By WILKIE COLLINS.

Armadale.	My Miscellanies.
After Dark.	Woman in White.
No Name.	The Moonstone.
Antonina. Basil.	Man and Wife.
Hide and Seek.	Poor Miss Finch.
The Dead Secret.	The Fallen Leaves.
Queen of Hearts.	Jezebel's Daughter
Miss or Mrs?	The Black Robe.
New Magdalen.	Heart and Science.
The Frozen Deep.	"I Say No."
Law and the Lady.	The Evil Genius.
The Two Destinies.	Little Novels.
Haunted Hotel.	Legacy of Cain.
A Rogue's Life.	Blind Love.

By M. J. COLQUHOUN.
Every Inch a Soldier.

By DUTTON COOK.
Leo. | Paul Foster's Daughter.

By C. EGBERT CRADDOCK.
Prophet of the Great Smoky Mountains.

By WILLIAM CYPLES.
Hearts of Gold.

By ALPHONSE DAUDET.
The Evangelist; or, Port Salvation.

By JAMES DE MILLE.
A Castle in Spain.

By J. LEITH DERWENT.
Our Lady of Tears. | Circe's Lovers.

By CHARLES DICKENS.

Sketches by Boz.	Oliver Twist.
Pickwick Papers.	Nicholas Nickleby.

By DICK DONOVAN.
The Man-Hunter. | Caught at Last!
Tracked and Taken.
Who Poisoned Hetty Duncan?
The Man from Manchester.
A Detective's Triumphs.

By CONAN DOYLE, &c.
Strange Secrets.

By Mrs. ANNIE EDWARDES.
A Point of Honour. | Archie Lovell.

By M. BETHAM-EDWARDS.
Felicia. | Kitty.

By EDWARD EGGLESTON.
Roxy.

By PERCY FITZGERALD.

Bella Donna.	Polly.
Never Forgotten.	Fatal Zero.

The Second Mrs. Tillotson.
Seventy-five Brooke Street.
The Lady of Brantome.

ALBANY DE FONBLANQUE.
Filthy Lucre.

By R. E. FRANCILLON.

Olympia.	Queen Cophetua.
One by One.	King or Knave?
A Real Queen.	Romances of Law.

By HAROLD FREDERIC.
Seth's Brother's Wife.
The Lawton Girl.

Pref. by Sir BARTLE FRERE.
Pandurang Hari.

By HAIN FRISWELL.
One of Two.

By EDWARD GARRETT.
The Capel Girls.

By CHARLES GIBBON.

Robin Gray.	In Honour Bound.
Fancy Free.	Flower of Forest.
For Lack of Gold.	Braes of Yarrow.
What will the World Say?	The Golden Shaft. Of High Degree.
In Love and War.	Mead and Stream.
For the King.	Loving a Dream.
In Pastures Green,	A Hard Knot.
Queen of Meadow.	Heart's Delight.
A Heart's Problem.	Blood-Money.
The Dead Heart.	

By WILLIAM GILBERT.
Dr. Austin's Guests. | James Duke.
The Wizard of the Mountain.

By HENRY GREVILLE.
A Noble Woman.

By JOHN HABBERTON.
Brueton's Bayou. | Country Luck.

By ANDREW HALLIDAY.
Every-Day Papers.

By Lady DUFFUS HARDY.
Paul Wynter's Sacrifice.

By THOMAS HARDY.
Under the Greenwood Tree.

By J. BERWICK HARWOOD.
The Tenth Earl.

By JULIAN HAWTHORNE.

Garth.	Sebastian Strome.
Ellice Quentin.	Dust.
Fortune's Fool.	Beatrix Randolph.
Miss Cadogna.	Love—or a Name.

David Poindexter's Disappearance.
The Spectre of the Camera.

By Sir ARTHUR HELPS.
Ivan de Biron.

By Mrs. CASHEL HOEY.
The Lover's Creed.

By Mrs. GEORGE HOOPER.
The House of Raby.

By TIGHE HOPKINS.
'Twixt Love and Duty.

By Mrs. ALFRED HUNT.
Thornicroft's Model. | Self Condemned.
That Other Person. | Leaden Casket.

By JEAN INGELOW.
Fated to be Free.

By HARRIETT JAY.
The Dark Colleen.
The Queen of Connaught.

By MARK KERSHAW.
Colonial Facts and Fictions.

By R. ASHE KING.
A Drawn Game. | Passion's Slave.
"The Wearing of the Green."

TWO-SHILLING NOVELS—*continued.*

By HENRY KINGSLEY.
Oakshott Castle.

By JOHN LEYS.
The Lindsays.

By MARY LINSKILL.
In Exchange for a Soul.

By E. LYNN LINTON.
Patricia Kemball. | Paston Carew.
World Well Lost. | "My Love!"
Under which Lord? | Ione.
The Atonement of Leam Dundas.
With a Silken Thread.
The Rebel of the Family.
Sowing the Wind.

By HENRY W. LUCY.
Gideon Fleyce.

By JUSTIN McCARTHY.
A Fair Saxon. | Donna Quixote.
Linley Rochford. | Maid of Athens.
Miss Misanthrope. | Camiola.
Dear Lady Disdain.
The Waterdale Neighbours.
My Enemy's Daughter.
The Comet of a Season.

By AGNES MACDONELL.
Quaker Cousins.

KATHARINE S. MACQUOID.
The Evil Eye. | Lost Rose.

By W. H. MALLOCK.
The New Republic.

By FLORENCE MARRYAT.
Open! Sesame! | Fighting the Air.
A Harvest of Wild Oats.
Written in Fire.

By J. MASTERMAN.
Half a-dozen Daughters.

By BRANDER MATTHEWS.
A Secret of the Sea.

By JEAN MIDDLEMASS.
Touch and Go. | Mr. Dorillion.

By Mrs. MOLESWORTH.
Hathercourt Rectory.

By J. E. MUDDOCK.
Stories Weird and Wonderful.
The Dead Man's Secret.

By D. CHRISTIE MURRAY.
A Model Father. | Old Blazer's Hero.
Joseph's Coat. | Hearts.
Coals of Fire. | Way of the World.
Val Strange. | Cynic Fortune.
A Life's Atonement.
By the Gate of the Sea.
A Bit of Human Nature.
First Person Singular.

By MURRAY and HERMAN.
One Traveller Returns.
Paul Jones's Alias.

By HENRY MURRAY.
A Game of Bluff.

By ALICE O'HANLON.
The Unforeseen. | Chance? or Fate?

TWO-SHILLING NOVELS—*continued.*

By GEORGES OHNET.
Doctor Rameau. | A Last Love.

By Mrs. OLIPHANT.
Whiteladies. | The Primrose Path.
The Greatest Heiress in England.

By Mrs. ROBERT O'REILLY.
Phœbe's Fortunes.

By OUIDA.
Held in Bondage. | Two Little Wooden
Strathmore. | Shoes.
Chandos. | Friendship.
Under Two Flags. | Moths.
Idalia. | Pipistrello.
CecilCastlemaine's | A Village Com-
Gage. | mune.
Tricotrin. | Bimbi.
Puck. | Wanda.
Folle Farine. | Frescoes.
A Dog of Flanders. | In Maremma.
Pascarel. | Othmar.
Signa. | Guilderoy.
Princess Naprax- | Ruffino.
ine. | Ouida's Wisdom,
In a Winter City. | Wit, and Pathos.
Ariadne.

MARGARET AGNES PAUL.
Gentle and Simple.

By JAMES PAYN.
Bentinck's Tutor. | £200 Reward.
Murphy's Master. | Marine Residence.
A County Family. | Mirk Abbey.
At Her Mercy. | By Proxy.
Cecil's Tryst. | Under One Roof.
Clyffards of Clyffe. | High Spirits.
Foster Brothers. | Carlyon's Year.
Found Dead. | From Exile.
Best of Husbands. | For Cash Only.
Walter's Word. | Kit.
Halves. | The Canon's Ward
Fallen Fortunes. | Talk of the Town.
Humorous Stories. | Holiday Tasks.
Lost Sir Massingberd.
A Perfect Treasure.
A Woman's Vengeance.
The Family Scapegrace.
What He Cost Her.
Gwendoline's Harvest.
Like Father, Like Son.
Married Beneath Him.
Not Wooed, but Won.
Less Black than We're Painted.
A Confidential Agent.
Some Private Views.
A Grape from a Thorn.
Glow-worm Tales.
The Mystery of Mirbridge.
The Burnt Million.

By C. L. PIRKIS.
Lady Lovelace.

By EDGAR A. POE.
The Mystery of Marie Roget.

By E. C. PRICE.
Valentina. | The Foreigners.
Mrs. Lancaster's Rival.
Gerald.

OGDEN, SMALE AND CO. LIMITED, PRINTERS, GREAT SAFFRON HILL, E.C.

www.ingramcontent.com/pod-product-compliance
Lightning Source LLC
Chambersburg PA
CBHW021110020726
47500CB00003B/694